BUMPO, BILL, AND THE GIRLS

•

KENT CONWELL

AVALON BOOKS
THOMAS BOUREGY AND COMPANY, INC.
401 LAFAYETTE STREET
NEW YORK, NEW YORK 10003

PRINTED IN THE UNITED STATES OF AMERICA
ON ACID-FREE PAPER
BY HADDON CRAFTSMEN, SCRANTON, PENNSYLVANIA

BUMPO, BILL, AND THE GIRLS

To Shea, my daughter, who has learned the secret of success, hard work. And to Gayle, my wife, the one constant in my life that has never failed me.

Chapter One

The sheriff paused on the boardwalk outside his office and watched the diminutive lawyer strut across the street toward the saloon. He shook his head and, for a moment, felt sorry for Bill Merritt. The cattleman had enough trouble facing him without some eastern lawyer bringing in more.

A grin cracked his somber face. "Yep," he muttered over his shoulder to his deputy. "If old Bill thinks three thousand head of slack-jawed, empty-headed cattle is trouble, wait till he talks to that runt going yonder."

The July sun blistered the Texas brush country, cracking the thick, gray soil; baking the centipedelike mesquite leaves; drying the water holes and creeks. But in the middle of Cibolo Springs, inside the Cattleman's Saloon, the air was cool and sweet. Three walls of the saloon wore a new coat of light green paint, recently freighted in from Brownsville for the general refurbishing of the saloon. A ladder leaned against the fourth wall.

Laughter broke out at the bar. At twenty-eight, rancher Bill Merritt could have bragged that he had roped, thrown, and hogtied the world except he had little in his pockets to show for it. He was cattle rich and money poor.

He slid a ten-dollar gold piece down the wet bar. "Set 'em up, Herm. We got to soak up enough to last three

1

months on the trail. Dodge City is a far piece, and we got three thousand head of ornery cows to nursemaid.''

A round of drunken shouts greeted his command, and a dozen bleary eyed cowpokes bellied up to the bar and grabbed at the bottles, splashing more whiskey on the bar than in their glasses.

They were priming the pump for a long, dangerous haul across the state of Texas, through Indian Territory, and into the middle of the dreaded Jayhawkers' Kansas. They had already spent weeks gathering hundreds of mixed cows from a dozen surrounding ranches, slapping a Box Slash trail brand on the bawling, cantankerous bovines, and trying to hold the half-wild beeves in some semblance of order until ready to push out.

One cowpoke, a redheaded lean piece of leather with the curious handle of Alkali Jones, gulped a shot of whiskey and washed it down with a mug of warm beer. Caught up in the revelry, he shouted, ''Whoooee! Ain't no man who can beat me on my feet. I'm faster than a hungry coyote and quicker than a stepped-on rattlesnake.''

His leathery face browned by the sun, Bill Merritt laughed with the rest. He held up his glass. ''Don't go blowing too much smoke, Alkali. I've seen many a rabbit outrun a coyote.''

''Don't hand me that foofaraw, Bill.'' He swayed on his feet and pointed a bone-thin finger at the grinning cowboy. ''You might be my boss, but I can spot you fifty feet and beat you at a hundred.''

Before Bill could reply, a skinny Easterner in a tight-fitting suit pushed through the crowd of boisterous cowboys. In one hand, he held a derby, in the other, a briefcase. ''Excuse me. Are you Bill Merritt?'' His head was cocked back, and he had to stare straight up at the tall Texan.

Bill brushed him aside. "Not now, pilgrim. It might be we got us a bet going here. Right, boys?"

"But . . ."

The roar from the grinning ranch hands drowned the skinny Easterner's words.

The rancher's grin broadened. He glanced around the saloon at the laughing cowpokes. His square face grew serious as he focused on Alkali. Bill cleared his throat and spoke in an exaggerated drawl. "Naturally, you being the whirlwind you claim, I'd have to have me a condition or two before I make a bet."

Alkali snorted. "Well, I sure ain't gonna tie one leg behind my back, if that's what you want. No way that'd be fair."

The saloon roared again, Bill one of the loudest. He held up his hands for silence. "Not that. Tell you what. Give me my conditions, and I'll bet you a round for the house I can beat you in a footrace, fair and square."

The lanky cowpoke shook his head. "No way you can beat me. Ain't nobody ever beat me in a fair footrace."

Immediately bets changed hands. Even money.

The skinny Easterner stepped forward. "Excuse me, Mr. Merritt," he began in a mousy voice. "I am . . ."

Shoving his battered Stetson to the back of his head, Bill ignored the small man who remained standing beside him. He crossed his arms and glanced around the saloon, a taunting grin across his face. He leaned back against the bar and addressed Alkali. "Then I don't reckon you got anything to worry about, do you?"

Alkali winked at a snaggletoothed cowpoke and gave Bill a smug grin. "Not from you, old friend."

There was another surge of betting, two to one on Alkali Jones.

"I still got those conditions."

The laughter subsided. The lanky cowpoke frowned. "Before I agree, what's the condition?"

The small man from the East interrupted. "But, Mr. Merritt, I . . ."

Bill spun on the small man. "Look, Mr . . . whoever you are. I'm busy." He hooked a thumb at Alkali Jones. "I got me important business here. Now, you just find a seat over next to the wall and be quiet." He pointed to the far corner. "After I pluck this chicken's feathers, I'll tend to you, you hear?"

Without waiting for a reply, Bill turned back to Alkali and eyed him shrewdly. "My conditions are that I pick the course, and I get a head start."

Another surge of betting evened the odds.

Snag Podecker, the snaggletoothed cowpoke, fished in his pocket, pulled out his last fifty cents, and waited. He had worked for Bill Merritt long enough to figure his boss was up to something.

Alkali shrugged. The course didn't make any difference to him. He could run on anything. "What kinda head start?" he asked warily.

Bill shrugged. "Five feet." He tossed down the remainder of his whiskey.

The lanky lean cowpoke guffawed. "Five feet? That's just one jump for me. I'll pass you like you was bogged knee-deep in a mudhole."

The odds jumped. Three to one.

"Then I reckon it's a bet, huh?"

Alkali balanced on one foot and removed a boot.

"Durned tootin' it is." He pulled the other one off and unsnapped his gun belt.

Bill Merritt remained leaning against the bar. He poured himself another whiskey. "Drinks for the house, right? That's the bet?"

"Ain't you takin' off your boots. You can't run good in them heels." Alkali laid his hat on the bar.

"Naw," drawled Bill, setting his glass on the bar and stretching his long arms over his head. "Reckon I can beat you with my boots on." He pushed himself away from the bar, stomped his feet a couple of times, and patted his handgun. "You don't mind, I'll just keep these on too."

The odds soared to ten to one against Bill Merritt. Snag made his bet—for his boss. He might be nothing more than a grubline cowboy, but he was no fool.

Revelers crowded around the two cowboys.

The small man sat in the corner, his hands folded in his lap, docile as a thirty-year-old wallflower at a Grangers' dance.

Alkali Jone's face turned bright red. "Just you get ready. I'll put that smart mouth to rest." He clenched his fists.

"Okay." Bill nodded. "You remember, I pick the course."

"Yeah. Yeah. So come on. You're frothing at the mouth. Let's get on with it."

Bill Merritt strolled lazily across the room to the ladder and stared at it. Then he climbed the first five rungs. He looked back down at the bewildered face of Alkali Jones. "You ready?"

Complete silence fell over the saloon as every last man stared up at Bill Merritt, flabbergasted.

"What the blazes you talking about?" Alkali frowned. "I said you could pick the course, not climb some blasted ladder."

Bill grinned. "This is the course. The top of the ladder is the finish line." He gestured to the bottom of the ladder. "Come on. There's your spot. I got me my five-foot head start. Let's race."

No one moved. No one spoke. Slowly, like the rising of the sun, the realization of Bill's joke dawned on the silent cowpokes. A tiny snicker sounded from the rear of the crowd. The snicker became a chuckle, the chuckle grew into a cackle, the cackle into hearty guffaws, and the guffaws erupted into shrieks of laughter.

Alkali Jones stood fixed to the floor, his face and ears red as his long johns. He clenched and unclenched his fists as he stared up at the laughing face of Bill Merritt.

Bill read the seething anger in Alkali's face. He leaped to the floor and clapped a hand on the angry cowpoke's shoulder. "Come on, partner. I'll split the first round with you. After all, it was just a bet."

For a moment, Alkali hesitated, but he couldn't resist Bill's amiable cajoling. His resistance crumbled. He grinned. "No, sir. No splitting. I lost, fair and square. I pay my debts." He waved at the bartender. "Set 'em up, Herm. Of course," he added to Bill, looking back at the ladder, "maybe I shoulda seen if I could have climbed over you."

They both laughed.

Just as Bill reached for his fresh glass of whiskey, a hand touched his arm. "Excuse me, Mr. Merritt. If you are finished with your little joke now, it would be in your best interests to allow me some time for a private conversation."

The skinny man in the tight-fitting suit stared up at him. Before Bill could reply, the man continued. "I am H. Albert Harper, senior partner of Harper and Harper, attorneys-at-law." He gestured to an empty table near the wall. "Can I speak with you for a few moments?"

Alkali backed away and faced the bar. The nearby cowpokes lowered their voices, deliberately turning away in deference to Bill Merritt and the attorney.

Bill turned back to the glass in his hand. He studied the amber liquid; he studied his thick, gnarled fingers grasping the glass; he studied his broken fingernails. Lawyers. They always meant trouble, and right now, he had more than enough trouble staring him in the face.

He spoke without looking at the attorney. "Look, Mr. H. Albert Harper. I don't like lawyers. I can't stand lawyers. And I don't want to be around lawyers. There's nothing you got to tell me I want to hear."

H. Albert Harper squared his narrow shoulders and squinted his eyes. His thin face took on the appearance of granite. When he spoke, the authority in his voice seemed to add two feet to his stature. "Mr. Merritt. Your feelings regarding attorneys are of no concern whatsoever to me. Please believe me when I say that I can spend the remainder of my life without mention of your name and be blissfully happy. As much as I detest exhibiting rude behavior and remarks without tact, your behavior demands it. I am here to tell you that your brother and his wife are dead, killed in a train accident outside of Boston."

Bill stared at the small man, who hesitated, glancing around at the now silent saloon as if he were addressing a jury. "If you wish, I can give you the remainder of the gruesome details in front of your friends. If not, I suggest we now take a seat at the table I previously indicated.''

Bill's eyes turned back to the whiskey glass in his hand. Frank, dead? The announcement dulled the anger that lawyer H. Albert Harper's sharp words had incited. Downing the drink in one quick gulp, the sun-browned rancher turned to the smaller man. ''After you, Mr. Harper.''

The lanky rancher stared across the table at Harper. ''Hard to believe Frank's dead. Never met his wife. After he left twelve, thirteen years back, he sent money for the ranch once or twice, and then I never heard from him no more. Figured he was probably dead.'' Bill declined to mention the animosity between him and his older brother. It was all in the past now.

Harper arched an eyebrow. ''No. He moved to Boston where he married a girl from a good family. He earned a great deal of respect back there.'' He paused and dug into his briefcase. ''But reviewing his history is not the reason I'm here. Frank Merritt is half owner of the ranch, the Two M.''

''That's right. Frank mortgaged the family farm to buy the land around us, about four thousand acres. We'd agreed he put up cash, and I'd run the ranch. We'd split ever'thing down the middle, but if that's why you're here, Mr. Harper, you're out of luck. I manage to keep up the interest. That's about all. The ranch is still mortgaged up to the neck. Fact is, me and my boys are moving out a herd of cattle to Dodge City come morning. If it pays off, we can get the ranch clear of debt.''

H. Albert Harper shook his head. ''That's not why I'm here. It's a matter of the will. You're named in it. Your older brother left you two of his most valuable treasures.''

Bill's heart jumped into his throat. Valuable treasures?

Harper quickly erased any dreams of wealth. ''He, and his wife, Willamenna, believed the West would provide them the maturity and independence they could not get back in Boston.''

Leaning back in his chair, Bill Merritt eyed the smaller man. He was confused. ''You talking about horses or what?''

For the first time, Harper laughed. He reminded Bill of the shy schoolteacher in town. ''Oh, dear me, no, Mr. Merritt. I'm talking about your two nieces, Linitta and Alwilda Merritt.''

''My what?'' The stunned rancher leaned back farther, and without warning, the chair legs slipped, and he fell backward. He hit and rolled over, ending up sitting on the floor, legs spread, leaning back against the wall.

His eyes bugged out. He opened his mouth to speak, but nothing came out.

H. Albert Harper continued in a flat, unyielding tone. ''Linitta is ten, Alwilda, eight. Both are bright and pleasant young ladies. As you are their nearest relative, they are entrusted to your care.''

''But . . .''

By now, the crowd of cowpokes had drifted from the bar to the table, mesmerized with the unlikely story unfolding before them.

Harper added. ''Naturally, the parents were aware of the decided lack of civilization out here. . . .'' He paused to look around the saloon distastefully. ''So they requested a nanny to look after the girls.''

''But—''

"The nanny will also continue their education."

"But—"

"Funds have been supplied. Frank guessed that the ranch was broke. He implied that he had never expected the ranch to make money under your care, so he did provide funds for essentials for the girls and their chaperone."

"But—"

Harper held up his hand. "I know this seems a bit unusual to someone like you, but I have thoroughly investigated the entire plan and I am quite comfortable with it."

Bill finally managed to find his voice. "Well, maybe you are, but I'm not. There's no way I'm taking on two female children." He rose and climbed back in his chair.

"But you're their next of kin, Mr. Merritt. Do you want them to go to an orphanage?"

"What do you mean, an orphanage. Didn't you say Frank left money for them? Put 'em up at a boarding school or something like that. This here is cattle country. Tough out here. Kill a jasper without thinking twice. No place for kids. Isn't there a family on his wife's side?"

Harper nodded. "Oh, yes. And there's a provision for that."

Bill grinned. Now they were getting somewhere. "Good. Let them take care of the kids. Like I said, we're kicking off with a herd of pure mean, ornery beeves for Dodge City. That's no place for two female girls and their nanny."

"You could be right, Mr. Merritt."

Suddenly, Bill hesitated, wary. Lawyer Harper seemed right accommodating all of a sudden. "I could?"

"Oh, yes. Your brother also made a provision in case you did refuse to take the girls."

"That's better," the rancher replied, relieved that he wouldn't be saddled down with two squalling girls.

The only family on the late Mrs. Merritt's side is a spinster great-aunt fifty-five years old. She will be returning from the continent in four months. She can take them off your hands then."

"Four months?" Bill punched himself in the chest with his finger. "I can't look after them for two days, much less four months. I told you that already. Can't you lawyers understand plain words?"

Harper ignored his entreaty. "Your brother's will declares that if you keep the girls until the spinster returns, the Two M ranch is yours, even if you turn the girls over to their aunt."

Bill started to protest, then he hesitated. "What was that again?"

"You heard me right." Harper stared at the rancher through shrewd, knowing eyes. "I am authorized to turn Frank Fletcher Merritt's share of the ranch over to you at the end of four months, but only if you have kept the two girls with you."

The idea was intriguing, inviting, irresistible. He studied the lawyer through narrowed eyes. "And you say, at the end of four months, I can turn them over to this old maid spinster, huh? Get 'em out of my hair?"

Harper nodded emphatically. "That's right."

Suddenly aware of the drift of cowpokes surrounding the table, taking in every bit of the conversation, Bill glared at them. "Get back over to the bar. This ain't none of your business."

He did some quick calculating. They had a nanny. So

there was nothing keeping him from arranging for them to stay right here in Cibolo Springs until he got back from the cattle drive. That would take just about three months, maybe four if he stretched it. Whatever time was left over, a few days, a couple weeks, he could handle standing on his head.

"Something I don't understand, Mr. Harper. My brother, Frank. Him and me didn't get along too much. Being the older, he naturally tried to boss me. That's where the trouble come from. I never figured he really liked me. So why did he send me these two girls?"

The attorney nodded. "Fair question, Mr. Merritt. Your brother believed the West was the tempering factor that made him a man. He planned on coming back and bringing his family, hoping to give them some insight into his own youth, and the hard life that made him so . . . well, so concerned about his own children. He had the foresight to plan for his girls just in case he was unable to bring them back to his ranch here in Texas. He believed a few months of this . . ." Harper glanced around the saloon and rolled his eyes. "Of this country would develop a deep appreciation within the girls of their life back in Boston. Provide necessary impetus. You understand?"

Bill didn't understand. He studied the diminutive lawyer. But the proposition was interesting. Why not? He could leave them in Cibolo Springs until he returned, put them up at the Widow Schmidt's boardinghouse. Sure. That'd work. He rose, stretched his lanky arms over his head and grinned. "Well, Mr. Harper. I reckon you got a deal." He extended his hand. "When do these two little females get here?"

Harper scrutinized Bill carefully, but the rancher kept

an innocent and unassuming expression on his face. The smaller man cleared his throat. "On the three-o'clock stage." He slipped his watch from his vest pocket and snapped open the cover with his thumbnail. "In thirty minutes."

Snag leaned against the bar as Bill and the lawyer left. A cowpoke by his side asked, "What's a nanny?"

"Not sure," replied Snag. "Reckon it's some kind of goat."

Outside, Bill stepped off the porch and loosened the reins of his horse as lawyer Harper headed for the stage office. "Come on, Bumpo." He led his horse down the street, falling into step with the attorney, who remained on the boardwalk.

Harper glanced at the rancher. "You must be an erudite man, Mr. Merritt."

Bill frowned. "Reckon not, Mr. Harper. I done a lot of things, but I never erudited anybody that I know of."

The attorney laughed. "No, I mean, educated."

"Oh." Bill shrugged. "I can read and write. Hope you don't figure on me teaching those girls any reading or writing. Maybe some numbers. I was right good with numbers."

"That won't be necessary, Mr. Merritt. I was referring to the name of your horse there. Bumpo. Is that it?" He stepped off the boardwalk and started to touch the roan.

Bill yanked on the bridle just as Bumpo, teeth bared, lunged at the lawyer. "Back away there, lawyer. He don't like people."

Lawyer Harper jumped back and stumbled over the boardwalk, noticeably flustered and frightened.

"Out here, Mr. Harper," Bill explained, "you don't

touch any animal except what's yours. This one here, he's what you'd call a strictly one-man animal, and believe me, I got a tough enough job airing him out every morning. This knothead would probably go wild if he ran free for two days."

Rising to his feet and brushing himself off, Harper grinned sheepishly as they continued down the street toward the stage office. "I apologize, Mr. Merritt. You're right, of course. I shouldn't have been so forward. Out here, different culture and all. What I meant was the name you gave him, Bumpo, is a literary one."

"Literary? You mean from books? That's where I got it. I read a lot. My favorite is *Leatherstocking Tales,* by some hombre named Cooper."

"Yes," said Harper, beaming. "I've read him. Excellent narrative. Breathtaking descriptions. Sometimes I wonder if it could be metaphoric."

Bill arched an eyebrow. He wasn't sure just what Harper was talking about now. Those lawyers knew a lot of words. Trouble was, most words they knew didn't make any sense to the average jasper. "I liked his stories good enough. He was wrong some about the Indians sometimes, and a couple other items, but I liked his stories. That's where I came up with the name for this ornery animal. Bumpo, after Natty Bumpo, though he was a man with some sense. A lot more than I can say for this jugheaded hay burner." Bill halted in front of the station. "Reckon the stage'll be in directly," he said as he tied Bumpo to the rail.

The three-o'clock stage rocked into Cibolo Springs at four-thirty and skidded to a halt in a mushroom of dust in front of the stage office where Harper and Bill waited impatiently. Behind them, a crowd had gathered, word of the two girls having spread through town like wildfire.

H. Albert Harper scurried off the boardwalk and opened the stage door. One girl, wearing a pinafore over a high-necked dress, paused in the open door, took Harper's extended hand, and stepped to the ground. The second child, similarly dressed, didn't wait for Harper. Instead, she jumped to the ground and looked around excitedly.

A young woman wearing a plain dark gray dress and a straw bonnet topped with imitation flowers appeared in the open door—the nanny, Bill guessed.

Harper escorted the three to the boardwalk where he made the introductions. Linitta and Alwilda curtsied, and the nanny, Millicent Deavers, offered her hand. "I'm very happy to meet you, Mr. Merritt," she said in a soft voice.

Bill's hand swallowed hers. He gulped. "Yes, ma'am. Me too. I mean, pleased to meet you." She was a sight prettier than what he had expected of a nanny. She had red hair, and her skin was a golden color, nothing like the pale skin of redheaded Alkali Jones. "You been with the girls long?"

H. Albert Harper replied for her. "Miss Deavers was employed by Harper and Harper especially for this job."

Behind them, the driver and station agent were busy loading and unloading luggage and freight from the Concord stage.

Bill frowned. "You mean, she's not with them regular? All the time? I thought you said Frank wanted a nanny to teach reading and writing."

A sly grin spread over H. Albert Harper's face. "Oh, that too. Miss Deavers is an excellent teacher, but part of her job is to also make sure you live up to the terms of your brother's will, that you keep the girls with you for the next four months.''

The stunned rancher's jaw bounced off the ground. He felt like someone had punched him in the stomach with a singletree. ''But I got me a cattle drive. What about the cattle drive?''

H. Albert Harper jumped into the stage and slammed the door. He stuck his head out the window. ''Good-bye, Mr. Merritt. I'll be back in four months.''

''But the cattle drive. What about the cattle drive?''

''Four months, Mr. Merritt. That's the deal. Funds for the children's care have been placed in the bank to use as you see fit.''

''Forget the money. It's the cattle drive, blast it. What do I do with the girls?''

Lawyer Harper grinned. ''Take them with you.''

Chapter Two

Long after the lumbering Concord stage disappeared into the thick *brasada* surrounding Cibolo Springs, Bill Merritt continued to stare after it. Finally, he turned to Millicent Deavers and his nieces. They looked up at him expectantly.

Behind them, an amused crowd had gathered. Word of Bill's bizarre obligation had spread through the small town faster than a starving wolf could gobble a chunk of meat.

Bill eyed the crowd with misgivings.

"I've got to go to the room." Alwilda looked up at the rawboned rancher expectantly.

Room? He looked at her, then at Millicent, and then at Linitta as the ten-year-old explained in a prim voice, "That's where the water closet is."

Water closet? Bill looked at Millicent.

"The toilet," she whispered.

Bill's face burned and snickers came from the crowd. He shot them a baleful look, and the giggles subsided.

Widow Schmidt saved the day. "Certainly these poor girls need to freshen up." She did a brief curtsy to the three newcomers. "My name is Wilma Schmidt. I own the boardinghouse across the street. You are more than welcome to use the facilities there."

Millicent smiled brightly. "Thank you, Miss Schmidt."

"It's Mrs., dear. Mr. Schmidt, he has been dead these last twelve years. He got drunk and passed out on a rattlesnake, best we can figure. Found the snake under him. He was a big man. Must have killed the snake when he fell on it, but not before it got its teeth into him. I buried the snake with him. It seemed appropriate." She paused.

With a brief nod, Millicent reached for the girls. "We do appreciate it, Mrs. Schmidt. Come, girls. Let's wash off the dust from the trip while your uncle makes all the arrangements."

As they stepped off the boardwalk, Alwilda pulled away from Millicent and ran to Bumpo. "Look at the horsey. Isn't he pretty?" She reached out her hand.

Bill leaped forward, knocking Millicent and Linitta aside. "Bumpo! No!"

He grabbed the bridle just as the girl's chubby hand touched the horse. To Bill's surprise, Bumpo didn't move a muscle except to cock his ears forward curiously. He remained perfectly still as the girl scratched his muzzle.

"Well, I'll be hornswoggled," mumbled Alkali Jones, one of the onlookers.

"Yeah," Snag whispered. "That broomtail's the orneriest cayuse I ever seen. And he's just standing there like he's got good sense."

"Sure 'nuff," muttered another.

Bill stared in disbelief.

Millicent brushed past him roughly. "You didn't have to run over us, Mr. Merritt." She looked at Bumpo.

Gently she scratched his muzzle. "After all, he's just a horse. The child won't hurt him."

Linitta joined in, and soon all three were petting Bumpo, who stood motionless, his reddish coat glistening in the sun. "Such a pretty horse," whispered the older girl.

"That's enough, girls. Let's go now. You can pet the nice horsey later."

A few snickers came from the onlooking crowd as Bill stood dumbfounded beside his temperamental stallion, watching the two women and two blond-haired girls march across the street to the boardinghouse.

After they entered the house, he stared at their luggage on the boardwalk at his feet. Arrangements? What kind of arrangements do you make for three women on a cattle drive? You don't. Women don't go on cattle drives.

Alkali sauntered up to him and pulled out a bag of Bull Durham. "What now, boss?" He reached out a tentative hand to pet Bumpo, and the horse laid back his ears and bared his teeth. The lanky cowpoke went back to building his cigarette.

Taking a deep breath, the broad-shouldered rancher slowly blew it out through pursed lips. "I'm not really sure. I don't cotton to nursemaiding three greenhorns for the next four months."

The lean cowpoke stuck his hand-built cigarette between his lips and touched a match to it. "That's asking for trouble, big trouble. Mark my words. I wouldn't do it."

Bill removed his Stetson and ran his fingers through his hair. He kept his eyes on the boardinghouse. "Well, they are my kin, but the big thing is, I do it, and I get Frank's share of the ranch. You got a better idea?"

Alkali considered the problem. "Nope. Nary a one. 'Pears to me, H. Albert Harper might just have you hogtied good and proper." He dragged deeply on the cigarette and blew a perfect circle into the still, hot air. "And you got no choice but to jump through his hoop . . . just like this." He poked his finger through the middle of the circle. A smug grin cracked his slender face.

The rancher tugged his hat on his head. He arched an eyebrow. "Not just me. *We.* After all, you're my *segundo.*"

The grin on Alkali's face faded quickly. "Yeah, but boss, I'm . . . and women . . . Besides, you know how Pancake hates women. He wouldn't want 'em out at the ranch."

Bill glared at his *segundo.* Pancake Poindexter had been the Two M greasy belly for fifteen years. He was cantankerous, foul-tempered, detested water except for making coffee, but he was also the best camp cook west of the Mississippi. "Blast his wrinkled old hide, if I want them out there, he'll get used to it, or I'll hire us another cookie." He nodded to the luggage. "Now, get a wagon and toss that folderol in it. I'll meet you down at the livery." He headed toward the boardinghouse. "I got some arrangements to make. We got a cattle drive coming, and that's no place for women." He would set them straight.

The widow's boardinghouse was neat and clean, so clean that Bill stomped his feet several times before he ambled inside. He glanced over his backtrail and grinned when he saw that he hadn't brought any dust inside.

"You can wait in the parlor, Mr. Merritt," said

Widow Schmidt primly. "Miss Deavers and her charges will be right in."

"Thank you, ma'am." Gingerly Bill sat on the edge of a velvet-covered wingback. He glanced around the parlor, feeling somewhat confined by the lacy curtains and fine, store-bought furniture. On the table next to his chair was a decorative lamp with a shade of colored glass.

"Mr. Merritt."

He jumped to his feet as Millicent Deavers ushered the two girls into the room. They halted in front of him and stared up respectfully. He held his hat with both hands and shuffled his feet. "Ah . . . everything . . . all right?"

Millicent Deavers replied. "Yes, thank you."

He looked at his nieces. Their faces were fresh scrubbed, and their eyes twinkled. They were right pretty.

The younger girl broke the silence. "Are you really my daddy's brother? You don't look like him. He was handsome."

Bill stammered, then nodded. "Why, yeah. I'm his brother, your uncle. And . . . ah . . ."

Linitta jammed her elbow into Alwilda's side. "Hush. Remember what Daddy said. Uncle Bill's kind of funny. Don't say anything that will set him off."

Alwilda glared at her sister. "Don't you tell me what to do. You're not my boss." She pursed her lips in a pout. "I hate you. You're always trying to tell me what to do."

Millicent Deavers stepped between the two. "Now, girls. Remember your manners. Your Uncle Bill is following your mother and father's wishes. He will take care of us, and we should show him our appreciation. You understand?''

For a moment, Alwilda glared at Millicent. ''I don't care. I don't like it here. It's hot and smelly. I want to go home.''

''Hush, Alwilda,'' Linitta whispered. ''Don't be rude.''

The small girl spun on her sister. ''You shut up. I don't have—''

Millicent's angry voice cut like a knife. ''Both of you be quiet, you hear?''

The girls looked up at her in surprise. ''I mean it,'' she said.

Alwilda tried to stare her down, but Millicent won the test of wills. The girl dropped her eyes. ''Yes, ma'am.''

''Good. Now, you girls hurry to your room. You need a nap after our trip. I'll be up directly.''

Without another word, the girls left the parlor. Millicent smiled at the rawboned rancher. ''Please excuse the girls, Mr. Merritt. The trip exhausted them. Now, what can I do for you?''

He blew through his lips. ''I don't know much about little girls.''

She laughed softly. ''I don't think you know much about anything except cattle, Mr. Merritt.''

He frowned, not knowing if he'd been insulted or not.

Millicent hastened to add with a smile, ''Don't be angry. All I meant was that from what I've been told, you've spent your life building the Two M for you and your brother. You haven't had time for anything else.''

Bill relaxed. A faint grin played over his lips. ''I reckon you're right. Out here, the fancier things sort of get lost, or not paid attention to.'' He scraped his foot on the floor. "But that's not why I'm here, Miss Deavers."

"Please. Call me Millicent. We're going to be together for the next four months."

"That's what I want to talk to you about. You see, I got me a mixed herd of three thousand cows we're pushing to Dodge City. Probably, they'll be two, maybe three herds ahead of us. That's no place for three women. We got rivers to cross, Indians to worry about, rustlers, bad weather." He paused.

"Go on."

Bill glanced around uncomfortably. "Well, I . . . I just don't want none of you to get hurt. You know, those two are just little girls."

Her smile faded. She arched an eyebrow. "Oh? I hadn't noticed." He grimaced at the sharpness of her reply. She added, "So, what are you proposing?"

He looked her square in the eyes. "You and the girls stay here with the Widow Schmidt at night, and if you want, ride out to the ranch during the day. I'll be back in three or four months. That'll be just about the same as me being around, wouldn't it? That way, you'd all be safe."

Millicent studied him several seconds. The smile faded from her face. "Yes. We'd be safe, but that's not what your brother wanted. As I understand his will, he wants those two girls to get some spunk and common sense, something he would have given them himself if he had lived. But he's dead, and now he wants his brother to give it to them."

Bill hesitated. That wasn't the way lawyer Harper explained it. "But the danger—"

She interrupted. Her voice was icy. "I don't know

what trouble there was between you and your brother, but I think it is shameful when a brother has to pay a brother to look after his children. Those little girls are of your blood.''

"That's just it," Bill replied, becoming angry. "I don't want them hurt."

Millicent's face flamed. She shot back, "You don't want them hurt, or you don't want to be bothered with them?"

He opened his mouth for a blistering retort, then closed it. He glared at her.

She didn't blink. The anger in her green eyes matched his dagger for dagger.

He slapped his Stetson on his head. "I'll pick you up later. The ranch is about an hour from here." His words were clipped and angry.

"Good," she snapped back.

Alkali was squatting by the livery door, puffing on a Bull Durham, when Bill stormed out of the boarding-house and stomped across the street. As *segundo,* second in command, of the Two M for the last twelve years, he knew Bill Merritt well enough to know the rawboned rancher had just come out on the short end of the stick.

Bill ignored Alkali as he strode into the livery and began barking commands at the hostler. "Get me a new Conestoga. I want it rigged up for a woman and two girls. I don't know what they need or anything. Some place to dress. Bunks. Whatever else you can think of. Just get it ready for me. I want it in three days."

He turned on Alkali. "Get out to the herd. I got to pick up the girls and that nanny. I'll take 'em back to the ranch.'' He nodded to the hostler. ''You going to be able to get that Conestoga ready in time, Corky?''

The wizened old hostler grunted. ''Try. That's about all I can do. What do womenfolks need that men don't?''

Bill Merritt shook his head. ''I don't know. Ask the Widow Schmidt, but just do it,'' he replied irritably.

Alkali spoke up. ''Three days? That means we got to hold the herd, boss. What'll the other cattlemen say?''

''So hold them. Move 'em to some fresh graze. Anybody complains because we're holding fast, tell 'em to cut their stock out.'' He jumped up in a buckboard and grabbed the reins. ''Now, get out of my way. I've got to fetch those women.''

''Don't be ridiculous, Bill Merritt,'' Widow Schmidt exclaimed. ''Your ranch isn't a proper place for a fine woman and two sweet girls. Why, you probably don't have a spare room for them, do you? That's not proper.''

Bill took a step back. ''Well, not exactly. We can string a rope across and hang some blankets. Won't that be proper?''

She huffed. ''Certainly not. They'll stay here until you're ready to push out.'' She folded her arms over her more than ample bosom. ''Of course, you make sure you have a proper rig for these young ladies.''

He shook his head. ''Corky's working on the rig right now, but I can't let them stay with you, Miz Schmidt, ma'am. I got to be with them. That's what the will says. That's what that nanny says.''

''Nonsense. Miss Deavers said that until you were ready for them, she would consider my home as yours.'' She turned up her nose. ''Besides, no woman wants to share a room with a bunch of unwashed, heathen cow-boys.''

She started to close the door, but Bill Merritt stayed her. ''Hold it a minute. I don't understand something here.'' He pushed his hat to the back of his head. He held up his forefinger. ''Number one, I wanted her and the girls to stay with you while we drive the cattle to Dodge.'' He extended his middle finger. ''Two, she says she can't, because that's not the same as me being with the girls.'' He unfolded his ring finger. ''Three, she claims they can stay here while I'm out at the ranch. That's the same as them being with me.''

Widow Schmidt nodded tersely. ''Yes.''

The weather-tanned rancher scratched his head. ''I don't understand how she considers your home my home one time, and not another. That doesn't make any sense.''

Widow Schmidt sniffed. ''It wouldn't, not to a man.'' She slammed the door.

For the next three days, the rawboned rancher pushed his drovers hard, trying to stay so busy he wouldn't have time to worry of his problems, but the problems refused to go away. They remained in the forefront of his mind. As quickly as he found a solution, he discarded it. Like it or not, he finally decided, H. Albert Harper had him hogtied.

He hollered calf-rope.

The girls and their nanny were going to Dodge City.

''Well, boss,'' Alkali said that night in the bunkhouse, ''At least you got the money Frank left for the girls. I ain't asking how much it was, but strapped like you are, it'll come in handy.''

Bill topped off his coffee with a dollop of Old Crow. "Naw. That money's theirs. I told the banker to put it where it would draw some interest."

"But Frank sent it to help take care of the girls."

Bill shot his *segundo* a blistering look. "No. Frank sent it because he wanted to obligate me to him, and I swore that wouldn't happen again."

Alkali held up his hands in surrender. "Okay, boss. I was just asking. That's all."

The anger in the rancher's eyes softened. "I know, Alkali. Forget it. I'm cranky as a winter-gaunted grizzly."

The next morning, they pushed out, three thousand mean-tempered, long-horned Bar Slash beeves, twelve drovers decked out in leather *chaparajos* of every description, a chuck wagon driven by an ill-tempered, muttering cook, and a spanking-new Conestoga with a dressing room and three bunk beds. A young Mexican caballero, Ramón Miguez, drove the wagon. Millicent perched on the seat beside him, and the two excited girls stood behind.

Looking neither to the left nor right, the rawboned rancher rode up to the chuck wagon. "Don't forget, Pancake. Ramón has orders to follow you. That Conestoga is a mite heavier than this chuck wagon. Don't get him stuck. We'll noon at the lake. Alkali says it's still holding water."

Pancake eyed the rancher. He worked a chaw of tobacco around in his mouth and squirted a stream on the ground.

"Don't say it, Pancake. I'm sick and tired of every lop-eared cowpoke telling me what kind of trouble women'll bring. Just do what I say and tend your pots and pans.''

The old greasy belly tugged his battered hat down over his eyes. "Yes, sir, Mr. Merritt, *sir!* Whatever you say, *sir!*''

Bill clenched his jaw shut and returned Pancake's fierce look. For several seconds, the two men glared at each other. Finally, the feisty old greasy belly jerked his eyes to the front and laid the reins across the rump of his four-ups. "Giddap there, Josie, Maude. Giddap. Least you got sense."

As the chuck wagon pulled away, a rueful grin cut through the feigned anger on Bill's face. He couldn't blame Pancake, nor any of the others. They'd never been on a drive with women. The idea spooked them. He chuckled. Heck, it spooked him too. He patted Bumpo's neck. "How about it, boy? They gonna bring us any bad luck?"

Bumpo stood motionless as the Conestoga rumbled past. Millicent Deavers, her red hair covered by a slat bonnet, kept her eyes to the front. Alwilda stared at him like he was some kind of insect, but Linitta waved. "Hi, Uncle Bill."

Bill touched his fingers to the brim of his Stetson. Linitta seemed to be a nice kid. The other one, Alwilda—she needed her pants tanned good.

Behind them came the point riders, and behind the points, the herd. Reining Bumpo around, Bill pushed the women from his mind and fell in with the herd where he felt comfortable. With luck, they would reach the lake by late morning.

Chapter Three

The first day out on every drive, the noon layover was more like a picnic. Everyone was still in an amiable mood, no one was too tired, and one of the punchers usually launched into a camp song.

After a solid dinner of camp potatoes and sourdough biscuits soaked with sorghum molasses, Snag Podecker of the first shift broke into an off-key version of "The Old Chisholm Trail."

One by one, the cowboys joined in, Shorty Wilson, Catman Johns, Pump Harger, Swede Johanssen, and the others, none of whom could carry a tune in a five-gallon bucket. Millicent and the girls pitched in, giving the caterwauling a somewhat dubious claim to music. By the thirteenth verse, everyone seemed to be enjoying themselves.

As the last notes of the song drifted away, Bill Merritt poured himself another cup of coffee and turned to the men. "Boys, you're all experienced hands. Just remember. We're not driving these beeves. We're just trailing them. Let 'em saunter along as they want. We'll cover fifteen, twenty miles a day. Now, I know those are mighty long and tiresome hours in the saddle, but that's our job. Look after your mounts. You each got ten sound horses. Try to keep 'em that way. Some of you here know what it's like to be caught in a stampede on a worn-out hayburner. We'll probably be trailing some herds. Talk was that Earl Simmons up in Webb County was pushing out a herd.''

Several cowpokes grunted. Snag stood up. ''When you plan on us hitting Dodge, boss?''

Bill downed the remainder of his coffee. ''October. With luck, early in October.''

With a mutter of approval, the first shift of drovers mounted and headed to the herd, relieving the second shift for its dinner. Bill waited for the incoming drovers, so he could repeat the same warnings to them.

At the rear of the chuck wagon, Pancake busied himself washing pans and cups, muttering to himself about just how hard put a camp cookie was these days.

To his surprise, Millicent and Linitta stepped to his side. Millicent took over the chore of washing the dishes. ''You have more important work to do than this, Mr. Poindexter. Linitta and I can clean this up for you.''

Pancake stepped back on his bandy legs and stared at the two females. He shot Bill a surprised look, but the rancher averted his eyes and paid close attention to the coffee he was drinking, although he kept his ears tuned for their conversation.

''No, ma'am,'' the cook said. ''That's man's work. You ain't supposed—''

''Supposed to what, Mr. Poindexter?'' Millicent brushed her hair from her eyes with the back of her wrist. ''We just want to help. There's no sense in us being a burden on you men.''

Pancake coughed and cut his eyes toward Bill, but the rancher was looking the other direction. He cleared his throat. ''Well, reckon that won't hurt none,'' he said, trying to be gruff. ''Just don't bust nothing.''

Linitta smiled up at the old man. "Oh, we'll be real careful, Mr. Poindexter. Don't you worry."

With a frown on his bewhiskered face, Pancake returned to the fire and put on another spider of biscuits.

Bill struggled to keep from smiling. And he had to admit, the women pitching in like this was mighty thoughtful. Maybe Pancake and the boys were wrong about the trouble.

"Help!" A girl's voice screeched through the noonday silence.

Bill jerked around and spotted Alwilda standing in the shade of a large mesquite on the edge of the clearing. She stood rigid, staring at a tub-size prickly pear at her feet. Then she began to scream in short, shrill bursts.

Before Bill could react, the whining buzz of rattles hummed above the frightened girl's screams. With a muffled curse, he leaped forward, palming his six-gun, praying he wouldn't have to shoot.

Behind him came several muffled cries, but he ignored them as he raced across the clearing, searching the prickly pear for the snake. "Stop yelling," he called out. "And don't move."

His words fell on deaf ears.

The whining of the rattles intensified, and a grayish brown head rose above one ear of the cactus, waving from side to side. A black tongue flicked out, testing the air. The head rocked back, then snapped forward, mouth gaping, fangs gleaming.

In midstride, Bill snapped off a shot and prayed.

The rattler's head exploded in midair, and the limp body of the snake was hurled aside.

The small girl continued screaming. Bill grabbed her and quickly searched for fang marks. He breathed a sigh of relief. Before he could speak, he felt the ground beneath his feet rumble.

By now, Millicent and Ramón had reached them. He shoved Alwilda into Ramón's arms and leaped for Bumpo. "Stampede! Get those wagons together," he yelled at Pancake as he jammed his foot in the stirrup and swung into the saddle. "Ramón! Get them in the wagon."

Leaning over the neck of the thundering stallion, he raced for the herd. Gunfire rang out. Over his shoulder, Bill glimpsed Ramón hurrying Millicent and the girls to the Conestoga. Off to the rawboned rancher's right, the Box Slash herd rumbled through the *brasada,* smashing a trail half a mile wide through the thorny underbrush, heading directly for the lake.

Dust from the pounding hooves filled the air like a thick fog, obscuring the low-hanging limbs of the mesquite. Bill lay low in the saddle, trusting Bumpo to avoid the drooping limbs that could crack open a man's skull or snap his neck like a twig.

More shots filled the air from the far side of the herd. Through the dust, he made out the lanky form of Alkali Jones standing in the stirrups and waving his lariat.

The dust thinned momentarily. Bill urged the galloping pony toward the front runners in the herd, hoping to drive them into the lake and halt the stampede. If he failed, and the herd looped back, it would storm over the wagons, smashing them to kindling.

Wicked thorns from the thick brush raked Bill's shotgun chaps. He pulled his six-gun and, as he came near the front runners, fired into the air. The herd, angling toward him, veered away.

The lead steers saw the fast-approaching lake. They

tried to swerve, but Bill drove toward them, firing as Bumpo drove his shoulder into the lead steer.

Suddenly, they were in the water.

Bumpo leaned forward, stretching out his legs before the impact folded them under him and sent both horse and rider into the water beneath the oncoming herd.

The lead steers stumbled and fell, causing the herd to come to a crushing halt as it piled up at the shoreline. Cows bawled and horses squealed as they were caught in the compacting herd, which quickly began spreading along the banks of the lake in both directions.

The stampede was broken.

Cowpokes shouted and cursed, forcing the frightened cows into a milling circle along the shoreline.

In the lake, Bill Merritt held onto the saddle horn as Bumpo swam in.

"Fourteen head, boss," Alkali said.

"Yah." Swede Johanssen chimed in. "That bane be much money, I t'ink."

Fourteen head. Three hundred dollars down the river. Merritt shot a baleful glance at the Conestoga. Millicent was not on the seat. She was probably in the back soothing the frightened child. Blast that kid. She needed to be paddled, not petted. Why couldn't she have stayed with the others? Now, because of her, they'd lost fourteen Bar Slashes.

Catman reined up next to Merritt. "Want me to see if any of the meat is good, Mr. Merritt?"

The angry rancher tried to push his frustration from his mind. "No sense. It'll be shot full of blood." He turned to Akali. "Get those walleyed bovines moving. See if we can quiet them down before nightfall."

* * *

The *brasada,* the brush country, of South Texas is fifteen thousand square miles of gnarled, iron-hard mesquite twelve to fifteen feet high, forests of live oak and spiny hackberry, and thickets of whitebrush, persimmon, and shrubby blue sage. The brush is so thick that flankers on one side of the herd were unable to see those on the opposite side. The herd itself acted as an adhesive to hold the drovers together.

Bill reined up in front of Alkali and indicated a narrow road with a grass strip down the middle. "The Siringo water hole is about five hours up this trail. Bed 'em down there. I'll be back as soon as I can."

While the two men talked, the chuck wagon and Conestoga rumbled past, stirring up small clouds of dust as they rolled up the trail toward the water hole.

"What about you, boss?"

"Going on past the hole. See what lies ahead of us for tomorrow."

Alkali's eyes looked past Bill's shoulder. "What about the women?"

Bill shook his head in frustration. "What about them? Just don't let 'em run off. Keep 'em in the wagon if you can, especially that small female. We don't need another stampede. We were lucky with this one."

"Don't worry, boss." Alkali swung his pony around and headed for the points. As *segundo,* it was his job to make sure every drover carried out his responsibilities.

Bill touched his spurs to the roan stallion, and Bumpo broke into a smooth two-step along the worn trail.

The level of the Siringo water hole was low, but more than sufficient to fill the bellies of Bill's herd. And silver bluestem, buffalo, and curly mesquite grasses grew thick and lush, offering good grazing for the herd.

Of more concern was the trail ahead. With a click of his tongue, Bill sent Bumpo around the water hole and back into the *brasada.* He eyed the country ahead of him. Better than anyone, he knew that despite years spent in the *brasada,* no one was ever truly familiar with the brush country. He had ridden it often, but in its very sameness, the *brasada* presented a formidable maze, one mile very much like the next, with few discerning characteristics.

Despite his efforts to remain alert, his mind kept going back to his nieces. This was the most darn-fool stunt he'd ever pulled, taking three women along on a cattle drive. But, despite such a moronic move, he still couldn't come up with a better solution—unless he wanted to give up his brother's share of the ranch.

Abruptly Bumpo pulled up.

Jerked from his musing, Bill glanced around. They were on the edge of a sharp fifteen-foot drop to a dry creek bed. He had expected the creek to be dry, but the discovery still brought a frown to his tanned face.

He headed upstream, looking for an easier crossing. Fifteen minutes later, he found what he had been looking for, a gradual slope to the creek bed and a gentle rise on the far side.

To the west, the sun dropped below the forest of brush. He urged the stallion down the bank and up the far side. He had about thirty good minutes of daylight before he camped.

Half a mile from the dry creek, he pulled up at an old burn dotted with blackened tree trunks stretching into the golden sky. Lush, green bluestem covered the fire-blackened soil. A startled rabbit raced through the grass, stirring up three more that exploded in different directions.

Bill studied the mile-wide clearing. Bumpo's ears perked forward. The roan stallion snorted and stamped his forefeet. "Me too, boy. Let's back out of here," he whispered, gently pulling on the reins.

Bumpo sidled backward, then Bill headed him deep into the brush, swooping in a large circle to put the clearing to the south of him. The country had been relatively free of Indian trouble the last few months, but such a clearing was a lodestone to any passing body of Indians.

The fire provided nutrients for the soil, which gave the new grass a sweetness that wild game traveled miles to savor. Many tribes regularly burned grass year round, staggering the burns so fresh, sweet grass would be available for game throughout the growing and harvesting seasons.

Any jasper crossing such a clearing was begging to have his hair lifted. A thoughtless hombre died a lot sooner than one who always observed caution, and that was a fact of life pounded into a Westerner's head from the very first day he could understand words.

Bill started to say as much to Bumpo, but the snort of a horse deep in the *brasada* caused him to hold his words. He pulled Bumpo into a thicket of spiny hackberry.

Shadows crept through the tangled brush on silent feet, slowly drawing a dark curtain over the *brasada*. He squinted into the thickening dusk. To the south, in the direction of the burn, muffled voices broke the silence.

Indians. But what tribe? Comanche? No. Not Comanche. Apache? Maybe. Tonks or Lipan? Kiowa?

He hunkered down in the saddle, hoping his outline was lost in the spreading tangle of the thicket behind him. From the fading sounds of the party, they were moving due south. Directly toward the herd!

The waning moon rose, casting shadows across the *brasada* in sharp relief. Just as Bill started to move out, a shout broke the darkness, then another. Moments later, a fleeting shadow shot through a clearing, followed by two more. Deer. Frightened deer.

More shouts echoed to the south. Bill grinned and pulled Bumpo back into the thicket. He waited, but no Indians followed. They must have killed some deer. One or two words carried through the still air.

He chuckled softly, guessing that the Indians were butchering their kill. He moved out to the west, wanting to put as much distance between him and the Indians as possible. Odds were, the party would camp for the night to roast the venison.

The tangle of underbrush and trees twisted the wind, whipping it in convoluted directions. A few minutes later, a thin wisp of woodsmoke touched his nostrils. His grin grew wider. He had guessed right. The Indians were making camp.

For another fifteen minutes, he walked Bumpo before nudging him into a slow canter. Gradually he cut back south.

From the position of the Big Dipper, Bill figured the time to be around eleven. Once out of earshot of the Indians, he made good time. The moon illumined the trail with a bluish glow.

Finally, he heard the soft singing of the night riders

circling the herd. As Bill drew closer, the nearest rider reined up and pulled his six-gun.

"It's just me, Snag," called the rancher.

The cowpoke relaxed. "Hi, boss. Ever'thing okay?"

"Yep." Bill studied the herd. "Good and quiet. That's the way I like to see them."

Snag chuckled. "Reckon they're a mite wore out. How's it look ahead?"

"Indians. About three hours back."

Despite the shadows over Snag's face, Bill saw the grin fade. The cowpoke sat up a bit straighter. "Comanche?"

"Don't think so. No bells, and you know Quanah Parker's fancy for bells. Figure maybe Apache, Kiowa."

"War party?"

"Hard to say. We'll stick an extra point out tomorrow. Keep your eyes open tonight. I don't figure we'll have any trouble. They were roasting venison when I left. Full belly and a couple shots of mescal, they'll bed down."

"You hope."

Bill touched his heels into Bumpo's flank. "Yeah. I hope."

He rode silently around the herd, nodding to the other two night riders. The camp slept peacefully. The banked fire winked at him with red eyes.

Unsaddling Bumpo, he gave the stallion a slap on the rump and turned him loose in the remuda. He stretched mightily and rubbed his balled knuckles in his eyes. "I'm sure ready for a few winks," he muttered. His bedroll was stashed in the chuck wagon. As he passed behind the Conestoga, a stream of water hit him in the side of the head, soaking him instantly.

Chapter Four

"What the . . ." He stumbled back, sputtering. "Who the blazes . . ." He wiped roughly at his face as water coursed down his neck and back. He heard a sharp gasp and turned to see Alwilda peering out the pucker hole, her eyes wide with fear. She held an empty wash pan in her hands.

Millicent appeared next to her, her red hair disheveled, her eyes filled with sleep. "Alwilda! What's the matter? What are you doing up?" Then she spotted Bill, angry as a wet cat. She looked back at the girl, saw the empty pan, then turned back to Bill.

A smile leaped to her lips, one she quickly suppressed. "Mr. Merritt, are . . . are you . . ." Her shoulders jerked and she muffled a cough. "Are you all right?" Her lips quivered and her eyebrows rose in amusement.

The sudden exclamations awakened several cowpokes who quickly took in the situation and buried their heads under their blankets to suppress their own laughter.

Bill glared at the child. He managed to contain the angry reply on his lips. Then he glared at Millicent. His ears rang, and words choked in his throat. He glared back at the girl. "I . . . You . . ." With a mighty groan, he clenched his fists and stormed toward the chuck wagon, glaring at anybody who looked his way.

A chuckle sounded from one of the cowboys. Bill

spun on his heel and once again glared at the inert bundles on the ground, but not a single, solitary bundle moved.

A couple hours later, Pancake stirred up the fire and put on the coffee. Bill, in a dry shirt, rolled up his bedroll and tossed it in the chuck wagon beside the gutta-percha bags of sugar.

Pancake gave him a sidelong glance but deliberately refused to meet his eyes.

"You got something on your mind?" Bill demanded, sloshing cold coffee into his mug.

"No, sir, Mr. Merritt, sir. I just do my job."

Bill eyed the bandy-legged greasy belly. He sipped his coffee and immediately spit it out. "Blast. It's still cold."

Placing a spider of sourdough bread in the coals, Pancake grunted. "Probably 'cause it ain't had time to get hot yet," he mumbled, reaching for a slab of bacon and unsheathing his skinning knife.

Bill bit his lips. He squatted by the fire and stared into the flames. Who was he fooling? This situation was of his own doing. He had no one to blame but himself. If he hadn't been so greedy for the other half of the ranch . . . But wasn't that kind of natural, to want more?

Yet Frank was his brother. He knew how much the ranch meant to Bill. Why didn't he just give it to him? Why all this nonsense about those two girls who, the good Lord knows, would be much better off back in Boston? They couldn't survive the rigors of the West. They weren't as tough as the children born out here.

"Coffee's ready, boss."

"Huh?" Bill looked away from the fire that had drawn

him and his thoughts into it. Alkali was standing beside him, offering him a cup of steaming coffee. "Thanks," he replied, rising from his squat. He glanced at his *segundo,* searching for any trace of mirth on the lanky cowpoke's face. There was none.

The night sky was clear, promising a blistering day without a single cloud to block the searing rays of the summer sun. The sky foretold sweat, boiling dust, dry throats, parched lips, and thin tempers.

To the east, the first gray fingers of morning began grasping at the darkness, forcing it aside. As the rich aroma of the boiling coffee drifted through the camp, bundles stirred, and mumbling cowpokes began rolling out. Another day had begun.

Bill told Alkali about the Indians ahead. "Put out an extra point. You and me, we'll ride ahead. I'd like to noon at that burn."

"Right, boss. Snag can *segundo* while I'm gone." The carrot-topped cowpoke hesitated. "What if them Injuns are still there?"

"Like I said, it was a small party. We're not looking for trouble. We have to, we'll give 'em a beef."

"Okay. You're the boss. I'll go tell Snag."

"And tell him to keep an eye on those women. I'll point Pancake in the right direction." Bill glanced at the Conestoga. A lamp burned inside, but no one had put in an appearance.

Linitta fastened a ribbon around her blond hair. "But, Millicent, I'm hungry. And it smells so good. That bread Mr. Pancake made yesterday was wonderful."

"Me too, I'm hungry," Alwilda echoed, turning her back so Millicent could button her pinafore.

"Well, I am too." She paused and pulled aside the canvas covering the pucker hole. "But Mr. Merritt is still at the fire. I don't want to remind him about last night."

"Yes," Linitta said, staring at her sister. "I'd be mad too if you threw water on me."

"It was an accident." Alwilda pouted her lips.

"You shouldn't have been up that late anyway."

"I couldn't sleep. My face was dirty. Besides, I told you. It was an accident."

Millicent nodded. She turned the small girl to face her. "I know, but you've got to understand. Mr. Merritt doesn't know anything about children, and certainly nothing about girls."

"I don't care," Alwilda said. "I want to go home. I don't like it here."

Linitta shushed her. "Not me. This is fun." She looked up at Millicent. "Do you think Uncle Bill will teach me to ride Bumpo? He's such a beautiful horse."

Millicent looked into the ten-year-old's blue eyes. She'd only known the child a few weeks, but Linitta seemed older than ten—probably, the young nanny guessed, because the child had to be a parent to her sister while their father and mother had been out traveling the world. "I imagine he will, once he understands us. But it's hard for a man like Mr. Merritt. However, sooner or later, he will come to understand us. Until then, we must try not cause him any problems. You both hear me?"

As one, they nodded. Millicent glanced out the pucker hole. Bill had disappeared. In the distance, she spotted him saddling Bumpo. "All right, girls. Let's go get some breakfast."

* * *

"They don't look Apache to me," Alkali muttered as he and Bill studied the Indians from behind the thick wall of underbrush. "They sure ain't Comanche though. Elsewise, them bells would be ringing," he added, referring to Quanah Parker's penchant for dangling bells from his horses, a deliberate slap at the ineptitude of the bluecoats' at finding Comanches.

Bill nodded. The camp seemed peaceful. Half a dozen families. None of the braves wore paint. Strips of venison were draped over bushes, drying in the sun. A handful of children ran about the camp.

"Don't seem they're looking for trouble, boss."

"That's what I was thinking. Check your sidearm just in case."

Bill kneed Bumpo into the clear and halloed the camp. Instantly the children disappeared, and five braves jumped up, rifles in hand. One, his black, greasy hair hanging down his back, stepped forward. He wore a tattered white man's shirt and a breechcloth. The others were similarly dressed.

They stared at Bill with dark, fierce eyes. He held up his hand, extending his index and second finger, tilting them slightly forward, the Northern Indian sign for friend.

He approached slowly, changing the sign of friendship to that used by the Southern Indians, both hands extended, the index fingers linked. Alkali trailed behind, his eyes searching the underbrush around them.

A second Indian stepped forward, returning the sign.

Bill squeezed Bumpo's chest, and the red roan stallion halted. The rawboned rancher sat loose in the saddle. He extended his left finger and rubbed it with his right, the sign for Apache.

The Indian shook his head. He cupped his hand and made a rotary motion with it.

"Kiowa," Bill said over his shoulder. He nodded and returned the sign. "White man talk?"

A second Kiowa, his head covered with a battered black sombrero, stepped up beside the first. "I speak white man talk much good."

The other members of the tribe suddenly appeared, realizing Bill's visit was peaceful.

"I have many cattle." Bill pointed to the burn. "I would like to feed them here."

The second Kiowa jabbered to the first, then replied. "This is Kiowa land."

Bill grinned. "No. I was here last night." He pointed to the west, then to the remains of the deer. "I saw you when you killed the deer." He held his index finger straight up and moved his hand across his body, giving it the jumping motion of a deer. "This country belongs to no one. I only wish to feed my cattle. I will give my friends, the Kiowa, a beef to prove my friendship."

Another round of jabbering took place.

Alkali pulled up beside Bill. "Why give 'em even a scrub, boss? Let's just run this bunch of redskins off."

"Naw. Won't work. They'd tag along and steal one here and another there. Could cause us a mite of trouble up the trail."

The Kiowa spokesman turned back. "Two."

Bill shook his head and held up one finger. "One."

The first Kiowa grunted, then nodded.

With a peace sign, Bill backed away, then reined Bumpo around. "Get back with the herd, Alkali. Drop off a beef when you get here."

"Whatever you say, boss." The lanky cowpoke wheeled around and headed back for the herd.

The chuck wagon and Conestoga made good time. Just before ten in the morning, they rumbled up the trail to where Bill was waiting. He pointed Pancake to the far side of the burn, then rode back to the Conestoga. Millicent was perched on the seat beside Ramón.

"Where are the girls?"

"Inside," she replied, loosening her slat bonnet.

"Good. Keep them inside. You go back too. I want all of you to stay inside until we stop."

"But why? What's wrong?"

Bill wasn't used to being questioned. When he gave an order, he expected it to be carried out, but he held his tongue, for now he had suddenly been made privileged to one of the more celebrated characteristics of a woman. "Because," he began, "there is a small tribe of Kiowas ahead. I don't want them to see you or the girls."

Millicent's eyebrows knit. "Indians? There's Indians ahead of us?"

The rawboned rancher sighed in exasperation. How could he make it any plainer? "Yes. There are Indians ahead. Mean, butchering, woman-slaughtering Indians. Now, do you understand why I want you to stay inside?"

"Heavens, yes," she said. The golden glow of her cheeks turned white. She spun around on the seat and disappeared inside the wagon.

Ramón curled his lips and arched an eyebrow at Bill. "Woman-slaughtering?"

Bill narrowed his eyes. "Just drive, Ramón. Just drive."

"*Sí, Señor* Merritt. As you say, I will just drive."

Satisfied, Bill turned back down the trail to meet the herd.

Moments later, shouts from the Kiowa camp cut through the heat of the day. Bill reined Bumpo around and froze. Standing in the rear of the Conestoga was Alwilda, staring curiously at the Kiowa Indians who were babbling and pointing at her as the wagon rumbled past the camp.

Cursing to himself, Bill jammed his heels into the stallion and raced to the wagon. By now, a few of the Kiowa braves had gathered on the trail looking after the Conestoga.

Bill shot past them, waving Alwilda inside.

The small child, thinking he was greeting her, waved in return.

Bumpo slid to a jolting, stiff-legged halt behind the wagon. "I told you to stay inside," yelled the rancher. "Get in that wagon and don't come out until I tell you."

Millicent stuck her head out. Bill blasted her. "Don't you women ever pay attention? Get those girls inside and keep them there. And don't come out until I tell you to." Without waiting for a reply, he wheeled Bumpo around and headed for the chuck wagon.

Pancake poked his head around the side of the chuck wagon as Bill rode up. Still riled with his boss, he rolled a wad of tobacco around in his cheeks, worked up a spit, and let it go.

With a precision resulting from years of practice, Pancake sent the brown liquid in a graceful arc to splatter right in the middle of a dried cow patty. "Yes, sir, Mr. Merritt?" He suppressed a grin, but he savored a degree of smug satisfaction when he saw the frustration on his boss's face.

Pancake had known what would happen with females along. He'd tried to tell Bill, but the hardheaded rancher refused to listen. He just made up his mind without asking nobody. So let him stew in his own soup.

Bill removed his dusty Stetson and drew his forearm across his sweaty forehead. "Keep the women inside during the nooning. They've done shown themselves to the Kiowa. No telling what to expect."

"Yes, sir, Mr. Merritt."

A flash of anger darkened Bill's face. "And stop it with that *Yes, sir, Mr. Merritt* business. I've got to do things I don't like, and you've got to do the same. It don't do any good to be sarcastical all the time. Besides," the angry rancher added, "I can always hire me another greasy belly." He jerked Bumpo around and shot back across the burn.

"Why, you . . ." Pancake choked off his words, but he felt his face flush with anger. He was halfway tempted to step into a saddle and head back to Brownsville, or maybe on up to San Antone. Let Mr. Merritt hash out the sourdoughs and beans. See what he thinks.

The nigh-leader pulled on the reins, jerking Pancake's attention back to his animals. "What's wrong with you up there, Maude?" he yelled, tightening down on the reins. A rabbit scurried through the grass. Pancake grinned. "You're gettin' jumpy in your old age."

A few minutes later, the old greasy belly pulled the chuck wagon into a patch of cool shade and dallied the reins around the handbrake. He rose in the seat and waved at Ramón, who guided the Conestoga into the shade next to the chuck wagon.

"Bill tell you about them females?"

Ramon halted his team. "*Sí.* Four times."

Pancake grinned. "One thing about him, he makes danged sure a jasper knows exactly what he wants done. Just make sure them womenfolks stay inside. We don't want no Injun trouble."

Millicent's head popped out from the Osnaburg canvas. She smiled brightly. "I'm so glad we've stopped. It'll be heaven to stretch our limbs."

Before she could turn to the girls, Ramón stopped her. "No, *Señorita.* Mr. Merritt, he says you and the little ones should stay in the wagon. I will bring you dinner."

"What?" Millicent's face contorted in confusion. "But why?"

"The Kiowa. Mr. Merritt don't want them seeing you ladies."

She saw the cook looking on. "Mr. Pancake, what is this all about?"

Pancake wiped the tobacco from his lips. "It's them Injuns, Miss Millicent. They act funny when white women is around. Bill, he just don't want to take no chances. He figures to head off any trouble by keeping you ladies outta sight."

A stubborn glint flashed in her eyes. "That's ridiculous. What kind of trouble can I cause?"

"With Injuns, trouble just happens, ma'am."

"I still say that's foolish. What can it possibly hurt if the girls and I just get out to stretch? We can stay right beside the wagons."

Her question made sense to Pancake, but the temper Bill Merritt was in now wouldn't stand for any exceptions. "That's just what the boss said for you to do, Miss Millicent."

"Please, Miss Millicent," Ramón said. "Do what Mr. Merritt asks. Pancake and me, we will have trouble with Mr. Merritt if you do not."

For a moment, she stared at Ramón, her jaw set. Then she relaxed, and a faint smile dimpled her cheeks. "All right, Ramón. We'll stay inside, but only because we don't want you and Mr. Pancake to get in trouble."

Pancake sighed in relief as she pulled back and closed the pucker hole. He glanced back across the burn and froze. Six mounted Kiowas were heading toward them.

Chapter Five

Millicent and the girls settled down inside the wagon. With both ends closed, the interior grew stuffy and hot, despite being parked in the shade.

Alwilda whined and fanned her face rapidly with her hand. "Why do we have to stay inside? I'm hot."

Linitta tried to explain. "The Indians, Alwilda. Uncle Bill is afraid the Indians might get us."

"He's just thinking out our own good," Millicent added.

A pout twisted Alwilda's lips. "I don't like it here. I wish I was home."

"Not me," Linitta gushed, her eyes twinkling. "I like this. It's exciting. Indians and all. We don't have anything like this back home. Besides, Uncle Bill might let me ride Bumpo sometime."

Ramón stuck his head inside. "Here's a surprise, Miss Millicent." He handed her a pan covered with a red and white plaid cloth. Millicent removed the cloth. The pan contained three fat slabs of dried apple pie. "Cookie said you deserve it for keeping us on Mr. Merritt's good side. As soon as the beans and sourdough is done, I'll bring it to you."

"Thank Mr. Pancake for us," Millicent said.

Ramón grinned. "Yes, *Señorita.*" He backed out.

Millicent unbuttoned the neck of her blouse. The interior of the wagon was growing even stuffier. How wonderful a breath of fresh air would feel, she dreamed.

A sudden commotion outside startled her. She heard Pancake and Ramón's voices, but the others she couldn't recognize. In fact, she couldn't even understand them.

A cold chill rushed over her. Indians! That's why she couldn't understand them. She laid her fingers against the hot canvas as if to hold them back.

"What the blazes is going on here?" Bill's angry voice silenced the jabbering.

"What's wrong, Millie?" Linitta laid her hand on the older woman's arm.

"Shhh." She touched her finger to her lips.

Damp strands of hair stuck to Millicent's forehead. Perspiration ran down her throat. She glanced at the girls. Their faces were flushed with heat, and their cheeks glistened with sweat. The pie sat untouched.

Millicent strained to make out what was being said, but the discussion was unintelligible.

Abruptly, the rear flap of the wagon was jerked open. Bill sat on Bumpo, holding the canvas. Beyond him, six Kiowa braves stood staring into the wagon. Behind the braves clustered several old squaws, broken and worn. "Don't say a word," he whispered. "Just go about your business. They just want to look."

Millicent gestured to the pie. "Do what Mr. Merritt says, girls. Eat your pie." She picked up a slab and took a small bite.

Alwilda whispered, "But I'm not hungry."

"Me neither," Linitta chimed in.

Millicent gave them a sheepish grin and swallowed. "Me neither, but we can't let them know we're scared."

She took another bite. It tasted like straw and chewed like wood. "Now come on. If I can do it, so can you."

Linitta stared at the fat slab like it was a rattlesnake, but she opened her mouth and bit off the tip of the pie.

Finally, Bill dropped the canvas back in place.

Instantly Alwilda leaped to the side of the wagon and pulled up the bottom of the canvas so she could peer outside. "They're sitting on the ground by the fire. Uncle Bill is with them."

Millicent and Linitta pressed up against her. "What are they doing?"

"I don't know. They keep looking at the wagon and waving their arms. Then they talk some more."

With a sigh, Millicent leaned back against the sideboard and wondered just how she had managed to get herself in such a fix. She shook her head and ruefully reminded herself that she'd asked for it. She had never been farther away from Boston than New York, and when the opportunity arose for this trip to the West, she had leaped at it.

Like all Boston girls, she planned on eventually settling down with a solid husband in a solid home and having solid children. Before she did, Millicent had wanted to experience some of the spirited excitement that was part of the West, to acquire an adventure that would always be hers, so that when, in the years ahead, the solid home and solid husband and solid children grew too solid, she would have memories to carry her through.

"Well, old girl. You got just exactly what you asked for," she muttered, half-scared, half-excited.

Linitta, who had burrowed in beside Alwilda to watch, looked around. "What did you say, Millie?"

"Nothing. Not a thing. What's going on out there now?"

Alwilda grunted. "Still the same. They're just . . . No, they're getting up."

Linitta peered back out. "They're leaving. They're leaving."

Moments later, Bill threw back the canvas. Fresh air chilled the perspiration soaking the three. "Might as well step on out," he said. "No sense in staying inside now." A faint smile played over his lips, so faint that Millicent wasn't sure if it was a smile.

Behind Bill, Ramón and Pancake were cleaning up the camp. They glanced at the women and grinned.

Millicent and the girls clambered down.

"Don't go running off now," Bill warned. "We're pulling out directly."

Linitta nodded and glanced around. She saw Bumpo standing beside the wagon, his reins looped over the saddle horn.

"What was that all about?" Millicent nodded to where the palavering had taken place.

"Not much," Bill drawled. "Just some bargaining."

"Bargaining? For what?"

Pancake grunted and quickly turned his head away.

"For you."

Her eyes bulged. "Me?"

"Yep. Seems like they never seen a woman with red hair. They wanted to buy you."

"They what?"

"Yep. Offered four ponies. That's a fair price."

She hesitated. Was he kidding her? "People don't buy other people like that."

"Indians do." Bill glanced around. Linitta was standing beside Bumpo, scratching his jaw and rubbing his muzzle.

Before he could yell at her, Millicent said, "Let her pet him. He won't hurt her."

It was Bill's turn to hesitate. "He can be mean."

"Maybe, but not with the girls. Remember back in Cibolo Springs? Besides, Linitta has her heart set on you teaching her to ride Bumpo."

From the corner of his eye, he saw Alwilda approach Bumpo and begin petting him. "I don't know about that. I'd have to figure on it."

Millicent smiled knowingly. "Then figure on it. It'd mean a lot to her. Now, back to the Indians. Why did they leave?"

"Huh? Oh, I told them you wasn't for sale, at least, not for four ponies." Bill paused, glanced mischievously at Pancake and Ramón, then continued. "I told them I couldn't part with my squaw for less than twenty-four ponies. They . . ."

"You told him what? How dare you? I . . ."

Bill shrugged. His eyes twinkled with amusement. "I just hated to see you end up with a bunch of Kiowa. You saw what their squaws looked like."

"Their squaws? Those old ladies? They looked like they were the braves' mothers."

"Nope. Oldest one wasn't probably more than twenty-six, twenty-seven. Indian life is tough. Ages a body like no telling."

He paused and grew serious. "Look. I had to tell them something. To Indians, a woman on her own is fair game if she can't take care of herself or if she doesn't have someone to do it for her."

Millicent's eyes blazed. "You don't think I can take care of myself?"

Pancake coughed, and she shot him a dagger look.

Bill shrugged. "I didn't say that. I'm sure you can, but this was not the time or place to prove it." He glanced at Bumpo and whistled. "We need to be pushing on," he added. "I'd like to make another six or seven miles before night. And do me a favor."

The young woman ran her slender fingers through her bright red hair. "I know. Keep the girls with me. Don't let them run around."

Bumpo hadn't moved. Bill whistled again. The red roan stallion looked around curiously, then lowered his head so the girls could get back to petting him.

"One question, Mr. Merritt, before we go."

Blasted knothead. Bill suppressed his irritation with Bumpo. "Shoot."

She nodded in the direction of the Kiowas. "What happens if they come up with twenty-four horses?"

He shook his head. "They won't. No Indian alive has twenty-four horses." He whistled again at Bumpo, and again the horse ignored him.

Millicent smiled, but hid it with her hand. She laughed inwardly. That's it, Bumpo. Make him suffer.

Bill nodded to the wagon. "Best hop in. Let's go, girls. Time to push out."

Linitta replied, "Okay, Uncle Bill. Come on, Alwilda."

Both girls headed to the wagon, and to Bill's chagrin, Bumpo tagged along after them. Millicent had to turn her back to keep him from seeing the big smile on her lips.

* * *

Bill rode ahead of the point men, Millicent's question tumbling about inside his head. What if the Kiowa did come up with twenty-four ponies? He had to admit, there was one brave who seemed mighty interested, but the Kiowa, at least that band, were dirt poor. He pushed the idea aside. Out of the question. Only an Indian chief could come up with twenty-four ponies.

The next few days were uneventful. The herd ambled north, grazing as it went. They found water every day, sometimes two or three times, a blessing for which Bill said a short prayer every night. And he never failed to add an extra thanks that the girls hadn't stirred up any more trouble.

During the second week, Linitta began sitting beside Bill during the evening meal, besieging him with questions about the cattle drive, how far was it to Dodge, how did the baby cows know their mamas, why did girl cows get horns, why did the nighthawks sing, and why did they call them nighthawks?

At first, he gave terse, short answers, but throughout the next several days, he realized she was truly interested in the drive.

"Couldn't we save time if we made the cows move faster?"

"Could," he replied, sopping gravy with his biscuit. "But, if we bed them with a belly full of grass and water, they're more likely to stay in one spot at night. No stampeding."

"You mean, like the first day?"

Bill washed the biscuit down with a large gulp of steaming black coffee. He chuckled. "Like the first day."

Linitta became a fast favorite of the cowboys. She was friendly, always smiling, and always willing to fetch a cup of coffee for a lazy cowpoke. Alwilda kept to herself in the wagon, refusing to mingle, always whining to go back to Boston.

"She's just shy," Millicent explained when Bill commented on her absence. "Besides, she hasn't forgotten you yelling at her that day with the Indians."

"It wasn't just her. It was . . . well, everyone."

"I know," she replied, her voice edged with sarcasm. "Just give her some time. She'll come on out."

"It's okay with me," he said. "Just figured it'd make time pass faster for her if she got out of the wagon some."

"Uncle Bill?"

The rawboned rancher looked down at Linitta. "Yes?"

"Can I ride Bumpo some day?"

At first he started to refuse, but he couldn't on the basis that Bumpo was a killer. With the girls, the stallion was like an overgrown puppy.

"Can I, huh?" Her blond hair was in pigtails. She looked up at him with hope in her eyes.

He glanced at Millicent, who arched an eyebrow. "Well, we'll see."

"Tomorrow, huh?"

"Not tomorrow. We got the Nueces to cross. That'll keep us busy most of the day." He rose and knocked the dust off his shotgun chaps with his Stetson. "We'll talk about it later. When work slacks up a little."

"Yes, sir."

He shot Millicent a glance. She shook her head. And

for some strange reason he couldn't figure out, Bill felt guilty.

Alkali found an easy crossing on the Nueces, and the next morning, the herd swam the river and pushed on toward San Antonio, leaving the *brasada* behind. From there, Bill planned to swing west a piece and hit the Western Trail, which would take them past Buffalo Gap, on to Fort Griffin, then to Doan's Crossing on the Red River. From there, they had two hundred miles across Indian Territory before hitting Kansas.

But first, they had to cross the Atascosa Creek, a tributary of the Nueces.

"Full of cottonmouths. That's what I was told." Snag Podecker looked at Bill with misgivings.

Pump Harger disagreed. "I crossed the creek half a dozen times. Never seen hide nor scale of no cottonmouth."

Bill spotted his *segundo* riding toward them. When Alkali reined up, he said, "Take Snag, and the two of you hightail it to the Atascosa and find a crossing. See if you can put a lid on that talk about cottonmouths in the creek."

"I've heard jaspers talk about them. Don't worry, we'll find out for you, boss."

That night, a northeast wind blew through the camp, stirring the fire, popping the heavy Osnaburg duck canvas. The women slept through it, but Bill sat up with the first gust. A light drift of clouds passed quickly overhead, blocking the moon and stars.

He slipped into his boots and tugged his Stetson on tight. It was a strange wind. But he'd seen them before. He couldn't be certain for another few hours, but if he was right, there was a big storm out in the Gulf of Mexico, and it could be heading straight toward them.

"Coffee, boss?"

Pancake handed Bill a cup. He sipped from his own while his keen eyes studied the clouds whipping past. "Woke me up earlier. Could be we got some weather coming."

The steaming coffee was so thick, Bill could have eaten it with a spoon. He drank about half, then nudged Shorty Wilson with the toe of his boot.

"What's up?" Shorty said in a sleepy voice.

"Weather coming."

Instantly the short cowboy was on his feet. There wasn't a trail-driving cowpoke who lived who didn't dread stormy weather. "Bad?"

"Not yet. Wind come up. Just want to keep the cows peaceable." Bill downed the last of his coffee and tossed Shorty the cup. "Choke down some of Cookie's panther juice and come on out to the herd."

"Okay, Bill."

The rawboned rancher saddled Bumpo and climbed into the saddle. He couldn't complain too much. The drive had been fairly quiet, but now the threat of a hurricane plus a river full of cottonmouths promised to stir up a little excitement for the Bar Slashes.

Chapter Six

After sunup, far north of the herd, Alkali studied the fast-moving clouds. Like Bill, he had seen them before, thick, gray, scudding across the countryside from out of the northeast like stampeding ponies.

"Funny-looking clouds," Snag muttered. "So that's what hurricane clouds look like."

The red-haired *segundo* tipped his sombrero to the back of his head and drew his forearm across his sweaty forehead. "Yep. The storm clouds move in a big circle. Like this." He made counterclockwise motions with his finger. "Right now, if I got it figured right, the main part of the storm is back behind us." He pointed to the southeast.

"How far?"

Alkali studied the clouds. "Beats me. Must be a big one for the clouds to be so far inland. Maybe two hundred miles."

Snag snorted. "Shoot. We ain't got nothing to worry about then, ain't that right? We're over a hundred miles from the gulf."

"Can't tell. Bill and me, one time we got caught in a big one, over near Bastrop. Wind and rain for four days. Heard later, two sailing ships was found twenty miles inland when ever'thing dried up."

60

Snag's eyes grew wide. "Go on. Twenty miles? You ain't stretching it some now, are you?"

Alkali looked at the younger man. He shook his head. He been a skeptical young cowpoke too, but after a few trail drives and a few times riding the tiger, there was little in this world he doubted.

As the day passed, the wind intensified. Alkali continued to check the direction, but it remained constant, out of the northeast.

"Not good," he muttered.

Snag frowned. "How come?"

Alkali reined up and stared back to the southeast. "It's coming straight at us."

"What about the Bar Slashes?"

"Bill can take care of the herd. He's probably circling them up now."

"Them clouds look like they're moving faster, Alkali."

"Yep. Purty soon, some of them winds can right nearly tear the shirt off your back."

Later, they spied a line of trees marking Atascosa Creek. Off to his left, Alkali spotted a well-worn cattle trail. Tugging his hat down over his eyes, he veered toward it. "There's the crossing." From the sign, he guessed a herd had crossed here six or seven days past.

Snag didn't reply. He was too busy studying the thick clouds racing just above their heads.

The Atascosa was low, lower than Alkali had ever seen it. He sat in his saddle, studying the muddy stream, no more than twenty yards wide, churning slowly toward the Nueces. The howling wind rippled the surface.

Without warning, a V-shaped wake broke the ripples. Alkali stood in the stirrups and squinted. Cottonmouth!

"Look at that, would you?" Snag exclaimed, pointing to several more wakes, all of which headed for a thick bottleneck of uprooted trees and flood detritus a short distance upstream.

Even as they watched, two more wakes appeared and headed directly for them. The sinuous black serpents paused when they reached the water's edge, their tongues testing the air.

Alkali calmly palmed his six-gun and blew their heads off. The sudden commotion stirred up a swirling along the bank. Black bodies rolled over and splashed, churning up the water for several seconds.

"There ain't no way you're gettin' me to cross this creek," Snag said, his eyes wide with fear. "Man couldn't get more'n three feet afore them things would be all over him."

Scratching his head, Alkali studied the ground beneath them. "Herd came right through here about a week back. Signs obvious. Reckon how they did it?"

Snag shook his head. "Probably hit it running. Took their chances."

Alkali pulled his pony around. "Not me. Let's find someplace else. One thing for sure, we got to cross."

Snag shook his head. "Why not just drive 'em around."

"You know better than that. You going to drive thirsty cattle along a river without lettin' them drink? Once they smell water, they'll run over anything to get to it."

Giving his *segundo* a snaggletoothed grin, the young cowpoke nodded to the north. "Don't reckon we need to worry about them cows gettin' thirsty. Look yonder." Beyond the creek, a gray curtain that looked like fog rolled toward them.

"Get ready," Alkali yelled, pulling out his slicker. "Here she comes."

The storm smashed into them with a vengeance. Snag almost lost the saddle with the first blasting gust. He squinted into the driving rain. The trees along the river bent almost double. Several snapped, sounding like both barrels of a sawed-off shotgun firing at the same time. Fear pumped into his veins. No way they could ride out a storm like this.

He muttered a short prayer and turned his head to the wind. The rain was so thick that all Snag could see was Alkali's yellow slicker before him, and that's what he followed.

The wind howled like banshees, ripped at his clothes like demons grasping for his soul, battered at him like ghosts screaming to be released from their graves.

Snag lost track of time, but he stayed right behind Alkali. Abruptly the wind abated, and the frightened cowboy realized they were in a thick stand of ancient oaks, some with trunks eight feet in diameter.

Alkali led the way through the trees as if searching for something. He reined up and dismounted, motioning for Snag to do the same. Alkali yelled above the wild screams of the raging storm. "Wait it out here." He indicated a hollow in a large tree.

Overhead, treetops swayed, and Snag imagined he could hear the thick trunks groan in pain. Following Alkali's example, he tossed his bedroll and saddle into the hollow, after which they tied their horses in a copse formed by half a dozen trees forming a semicircle.

The rain came in blinding gusts, whipping through the limbs and wrapping around the thick trunks. With an effort, they lashed a tarp between the trees, forming a windbreak for the ponies. "It ain't no barn, but it'll work just fine for them," Alkali yelled above the howling of the wind.

Snag nodded and ducked his head against the storm as he headed back to their own shelter. The hollow was small but dry. Snag rolled up in his blankets and after a few minutes managed to work out a comfortable spot while the storm howled only inches away.

"Well, it ain't a hotel, but it's better'n riding around outside," Alkali drawled, fishing a strip of jerky from his pocket and offering some to Snag. "We'll just hang in here till it's over."

"What about the herd?"

Alkali didn't reply. He was wondering about it also.

"We must've been doing something right," Bill muttered, standing under the fly of the chuck wagon, sipping coffee. The Conestoga sat next to the chuck wagon, offering a buttress against the howling wind. The heavy Osnaburg duck canvas on the side of the women's wagon had been raised and knotted to the fly of the chuck wagon, creating a canvas arbor where weary cowpokes could stumble in out of the weather and grab a cup of Pancake's panther juice.

Pancake agreed. "Lucky we was near this thicket," he said, nodding to the thick stand of live oaks surrounding them. "Breaks up the wind."

Earlier, as the storm began to intensify, Bill had spotted the thicket near the base of a hill, below which spread a large basin, surrounded on three sides by low ridges. Quickly the herd was driven into the basin and the wagons parked in the thicket where the combination of trees and hills tempered the hurricane-force gales. Ramón and

Pancake had reinforced the interior of the wagons and added another layer of Osnaburg duck canvas to the tops, staking the bottom in the ground.

"A natural corral," Bill said, nodding to the basin holding the herd below them. "We got lucky." The wind and rain slackened for a moment, revealing a dark figure on a nearby hill. Bill blinked his eyes, and the figure was gone. He peered into the rain. It was probably nothing but his imagination.

Millicent and Linitta watched from inside the Conestoga. Alwilda lay on the floor, her head covered with a heavy quilt. "Will . . . will this last long, Uncle Bill?" Linitta asked.

He looked around at his charges. Linitta waited expectantly. He gave her a reassuring grin. "It might, but you don't worry. We're above any flooding, and we got plenty of grub." He cut his eyes to the canvas over their heads. "We're in a good spot in these trees and behind the hill. Let it do its worst. We'll be here when it's over. We might get wet, but we'll be here." He winked at her. She gave him a weak grin.

He glanced at Millicent. Her face was drawn. He poured another cup of coffee and handed it to her. "This'll warm you up some."

"Thanks." Her lips quivered.

Bill grinned. "I've been through these before. Like I said, we're in good shape. 'Course, you might get a little wet, but you can always dry out."

"We got plenty of wood in the possum belly," Pancake chimed in. "An' if we run out, Ramón here can get us some more."

* * *

Over the next two days, the winds slowly shifted from the northeast to the south and finally to the southwest. Everything was water-soaked, from saddles to socks, from boots to blankets, from tempers to toes.

Men rode for hours, fighting the driving rain and howling winds. Numbed by exhaustion, they slept in the saddle and mechanically climbed aboard a new pony every few hours. Their faces grew gaunt, their eyes hollow, their stomachs empty, but to a man jack, they looked after their cattle.

The one constant throughout the storm was Pancake's panther juice. The wetter everyone became, the thicker he made the coffee until near the end of the storm, it was so thick Bill thought about using it as a grease for the axles.

Swede Johanssen laughed, bringing a rush of color to his pale cheeks. "No. I don't t'ink dis juice is t'at t'ick, boss."

Catman Johns wiped his hand across his heavy beard. His sunken eyes twinkled mischievously. "Don't know about that, Swede. This stuff 'pears to be thicker'n that adobe mud down in Mexico."

Millicent and Linitta did what they could to help about the camp. Alwilda remained in the Conestoga, whining constantly, a behavior not lost on Bill. "Is she sick?" he asked Millicent.

"No. Not really. She's homesick. This is nothing like she expected. At least, that's what Linitta tells me. When they left Boston, they thought they were going on a nice little vacation."

Bill shook his head, feeling a touch of sympathy for the girl. "No such thing as vacation out here," he replied. "What about you? You seem to be holding up okay, Miss Millicent."

Her tawny skin colored. "Please, call me Millie. Millicent makes me sound like an old woman. And yes, I'm fine. Of course, I've got to admit, this has been an eye-opening experience for me as well."

"Oh?" Bill poured a cup of coffee and offered it to her.

With a gracious nod, she took the coffee, juggled the hot mug in her hands momentarily, then explained. "I'd never traveled, never left Boston. This was to be a once-in-a-lifetime adventure for me."

Bill arched an eyebrow. "Adventure, huh? Reckon I never thought about hard work being an adventure."

Millie laughed. "I'm beginning to see what you mean, Mr. Merritt."

"Bill. If I'm going to call you Millie, then I'm Bill."

She ducked her head, and Bill could have sworn he saw a touch of color on her cheeks. "Okay, Bill."

"How's she doing? The older one, Linitta?"

Millie gave him a knowing smile. "She'll make you a good little Western girl if you give her the chance."

Her words surprised him. "Me? What do you mean?"

"I'm not real sure just what you think a woman out here should be like. But I can tell you that girl has not uttered one single word of complaint. She's always defended you against Alwilda, and I've not seen her shirk any task she's been given."

"Task? What tasks? She doesn't have anything to do."

"Maybe not from you, but she looks for them. Ask Mr. Pancake. She warts him to death trying to help."

Bill glanced at the girl who was pulling out a piece

of wood from the possum belly under the chuck wagon. For the first time, he studied her while she placed the wood in the fire and expertly rearranged the coals. He shrugged. Maybe when they hit a slow day, he would let her ride Bumpo. Still, he reminded himself, trail life would be a heap easier if he didn't have to worry about the womenfolk.

The morning of the third day dawned clear and bright.

Bill stared at the rising sun wearily. His shoulders sagged, and his eyes burned from two days without more than a fifteen-minute stretch of sleep in the saddle. "Well, Pancake. A new day's coming. Reckon you can throw something together without too much water in it now?"

The cantankerous old greasy belly grunted. "You don't have to eat it," he shot back.

Bill chuckled and downed the last of his coffee. He climbed into the saddle and groaned. "We'll rest up here today. Dry out best we can and move out early in the morning."

"What about Alkali and Snag?"

"They'll be along," Bill replied, looking to the north. "One thing about Alkali, he hates water. I wouldn't be surprised if he didn't find someplace to hole up nice and dry through the whole blasted storm."

Miles to the north, near the Atascosa, Alkali and Snag crawled out of the tree hollow and stretched. The red-haired cowpoke grinned and scratched at his three-day-old beard. "I almost feel guilty spending the last few days loafing around like we done."

Snag nodded and glanced back at the hollow that had

been their home for two days. They'd managed to build a small fire and boil some jerky broth, and all the while remain nice and dry. "Well, old friend, you feel guilty for both of us. Me, it was a right pleasant two days. Cramped a little, but for the most part, I'd do it again."

The two cowpokes saddled up and rode back to the Atascosa, which had rolled over its banks and churned toward the Nueces. Alkali grinned. "Could be a stroke of luck for us, you know?"

"How's that?"

"Wash them away."

Snag frowned, then he grinned. "Hey. I didn't think of that. Yeah, I'll bet you a double eagle you're right." He stared at the swiftly moving water. "Fast as it's moving, it'll scour the creek bed clean."

Alkali reined around and headed back to the herd. "Let's go tell the boss."

Bill sat astride Bumpo on the south side of the herd, watching the cows search for graze in the mud. Three days had reduced the basin to nothing more than ankle-deep sludge, and some of the cattle were growing restless.

Shorty Wilson rode up. "We might have some trouble tonight, boss. No graze left."

Bill stared at the hill beyond the camp. "I noticed that. Reckon we best push them over the hill yonder. Fill their bellies and keep 'em content. Go ahead, Shorty. Move 'em out."

At that moment, two riders topped the hill, paused, then swung in Bill's direction. Shorty hesitated. Bill waved him on.

Minutes later, Alkali and Snag reined up. "Like we heard, Bill. Cottonmouths thicker'n dog fleas."

"Yep, but the rain put the creek out of its banks," Snag said. "We're guessing that it washed them away."

Bill turned back to Alkali. "Think so?"

"Could be, boss. The river was low, barely moving. I figure that's why there was so many of them. I tell you, Bill, I never seen the like of them. But after the storm, that water's moving faster'n a runaway buckboard. Only way any of them snakes be left is if they tied theyselves in a knot around a tree trunk. And then, they'd probably got beaten to death."

"Good job, boys. Now give me a hand. We're pushing the Bar Slashes over the hill for tonight. We'll move out at first light."

Chapter Seven

By the time the sun rose in a clear sky the next morning, the herd had already made a mile, slogging across a soggy savanna, churning the grass and soil into a muddy soup. The sun climbed higher, baking Bill's shoulders and pulling moisture from the ground in thick, cloying vapors.

Millie sat on the seat beside Ramón. Both girls stood behind her, bareheaded, collars open, foreheads glistening with a sheen of perspiration. "This heat is horrible," she muttered, opening her collar and fanning her face and throat with her hand.

"*Sí, Señorita,*" Ramón replied. "It will be even hotter. The sun, it dries the ground, and the air, it is like the river."

Bill rode up. "Best wear your bonnets, girls. That sun will fry your brains directly."

Millie forced a weak smile. She fanned harder. "It's suffocating."

"Yep," he replied, nodding. "There's so much water in the air this whole countryside is like a giant steam-room." He gestured to the broad savannas ahead of them. "On the ridges, you'll catch a gust of wind. That'll help. In the meantime, you best keep your collars buttoned, shirtsleeves down, and hats on."

Dutifully they followed his instructions as he rode off.

Alwilda screwed up her face. "He's mean. I'm hot. Why do we have to button our collars, Millie?"

Millie shrugged. Her tawny skin was flushed with the heat. "I don't know for sure. It's what your Uncle Bill said to do."

The smaller girl snorted. "Well, it sounds dumb to me."

Ramón looked around. "He is right. Look at me." He pointed to his buttoned collar and cuffs. His shirt clung to his back. "When I sweat, I stay cool." He tugged at his collar as if trying to pull something from under it. "The cool air stays in my shirt. It has no way out."

Alwilda shook her head and tossed her bonnet in the back. "That's silly."

Linitta buttoned her collar. "Do what Uncle Bill said, Alwilda. He knows what he's talking about."

The younger girl stared at her sister defiantly. "I will not, and you can't make me. You're not my boss."

Millie spun on the seat. "Alwilda! You do what you're told."

Alwilda's eyes blazed, and she set her jaw in determination. "No. I won't."

"Then you get in the back and stay there."

For several seconds, the girl glared at Millie.

"I mean it," Millie snapped. "If you can't do what you're told, then you get in the back and stay there until I tell you to come out."

Alwilda's bottom lip quivered, her eyes welled with tears, but she refused to cry. "All right. See if I care. I just want to go home." She stormed to the rear of the Conestoga, yanking the end flap down after her.

Ramón glanced over his shoulder. He arched an eyebrow, then turned back to his own business.

*   *   *

Midafternoon of the following day, the herd halted at the floodwaters of the Atascosa, which appeared to be about a hundred yards wide. Bill and Alkali studied the river and the graze about them. "This grass won't last long," Bill said.

Alkali drew his forearm across his sweaty forehead. "Reckon you're right. He pointed to the line of debris deposited by the receding waters. But it looks like the river's dropped a couple feet since we was here. According to Snag, the headwaters is purty flat country. That means we ain't going to keep getting run off, so the river oughta drop fast."

Bill searched the floodwaters for any sign of snakes, but all he saw were occasional limbs and branches caught up in the churning water. He reined Bumpo around. "We'll bed down here. See what it's like in the morning. Meantime, ride upriver. See if you can find a crossing in case we have to push 'em around.

The first of the herd splashed into the water, which was only inches deep, and began to drink. Bill whistled at Shorty and Catman. "Stay between them and the river." He nodded to the middle of the flood. "Alkali says there's about a six-foot dropoff somewhere out there."

The sudden bawling of a frightened cow punctuated his warning. "Blast," Bill exclaimed, grabbing his lariat when he spotted a wide-eyed beef caught up in the churning waters and being swept downstream. He jammed his heels into Bumpo's flanks and the roan stallion raced downriver, instinctively remaining in the shallow water less than fetlock deep.

Bumpo and Bill moved as one, the rancher standing

in the stirrups, completely trusting in his stallion. Bill shook out a dog loop and whirled it over his head, at the same time nudging the galloping stallion closer to the hidden dropoff.

Bumpo responded immediately, now splashing through water a foot deep. Bill waited, hoping the current would push the cow toward the shore, but it seemed to be doing the very opposite, instead carrying the bawling animal toward the middle of the river.

"Come on, boy," he muttered, whirling his lasso faster. "Get me just a little closer."

With a surge of power, Bumpo leaped forward, and Bill released the lariat. With unerring accuracy, the loop whistled through the air and slapped over the cow's horns.

Immediately Bumpo sat back on his haunches, setting the loop and jerking the squawling cow toward the shore.

"Watch those knotheaded cows close, boys," Bill said as he rewound his rope. "Come morning, if we're lucky, the water will be below the dropoff."

The water dropped quicker than Alkali predicted.

The next morning, Atascosa Creek was back in its banks. Bill had stopped by the Conestoga and explained the details of the crossing to Millie and the girls, after which he rode back to the creek bank, where he studied the receding water.

Alkali pulled up beside him. "What do you think, boss?"

Bill scanned the muddy stream for snakes. Had it just been him and the cattle, he wouldn't hesitate, but now he had three women, and that made a heap of difference.

He urged Bumpo knee deep into the creek and stopped. His eyes scanned the water. Nothing.

Without taking his eyes off the creek, he gave Alkali his orders. "Put Shorty and Pump on the banks with Winchesters. I'm going across. If it's clear, send the wagons one at a time with a couple riders—the Conestoga first."

"The Conestoga?"

"Yep. I want to get Millie and the girls over fast. If there's any cottonmouths left around, the commotion might start drawing them down. I'd sooner worry about the cows than the girls." He grinned and added. "And Pancake's too ornery for them snakes to mess with."

Alkali chuckled. "You bet." He wheeled about and barked out the orders.

Bill waited. Moments later, Pump and Shorty reined up on either side of the crossing. Taking a deep breath, Bill palmed his revolver and squeezed his knees. Bumpo stepped into the creek, his ears perked forward, the muscles of his great body wound tight.

Behind him, Bill heard the clack of metal against metal as cartridges were levered into chambers and hammers cocked. The water rose, touching his boot soles first, then creeping on up his leg.

He hoped the crossing was not so deep that the wagons would have to float. At that moment, Bumpo dropped deeper into the swirling waters and began swimming powerfully. Bill struggled to remain in the saddle. His breathing grew ragged. Sweat beaded on his forehead as his eyes continued searching the river for the dreaded V-shaped wake of an attacking cottonmouth.

Moments later, Bumpo's hooves touched the ground,

and he lunged toward the bank, scrabbling for solid footing on the muddy bed.

Suddenly, a rifle boomed, and a geyser of water erupted several feet upriver. Bill jerked around. He held his breath. His eyes flashed, searching the creek frantically for the snake. Where was it? A black object appeared in the water. He raised his six-gun, then relaxed. It was only a stick. He yelled over his shoulder, "Driftwood. Don't shoot."

Upon reaching the bank, Bill looked back across the creek. Millie and the girls were looking on. Even at such a distance, Bill could see the fear in their eyes.

Shorty and Pump remained on the banks, Winchesters cocked, ready to fire. Catman and Swede took their places on either side of the Conestoga and flipped lassos around the rear axle.

Alkali waved.

"Bring 'em on," yelled Bill. "Bring 'em on."

Ramón popped the reins and the team threw their shoulders into the collars. Catman and Swede drove their ponies into the creek.

Bill rode upstream, searching for any sign of cottonmouths, but he saw nothing. He turned back just as the Conestoga emerged from the creek, water dripping from its frame. On the far side of the creek, Pancake waited at the water's edge. Catman and Swede popped their lassos free and headed back for the chuck wagon.

Bill and Alkali's eyes met across the creek. The rancher holstered his six-gun and waved the herd forward.

During the nooning, Alwilda tagged after her sister and jabbered incessantly about the creek crossing. "I was scared," she said as Linitta searched outside the camp for firewood to restock the possum belly, from which most of the wood had been washed during the crossing.

"Me too, but Uncle Bill was right. He told us just to hold tight and not scream."

"I know, but when water started into the wagon, I thought we would sink."

Linitta handed Alwilda a length of firewood. "Here. You carry this."

The younger girl took the wood without a word of argument. "You know, Uncle Bill isn't all that dumb."

Linitta arched an eyebrow. "That's what Millie has been trying to tell you, silly. Uncle Bill just has a lot on his mind taking care of all those cows."

Alwilda shrugged. "Well, he doesn't have to yell at me all the time."

"Don't be a ninny. Last time he yelled was about the Indians. That was a long time ago."

"Well," she replied, "he shouldn't have yelled at me then. Father never yelled at me."

Linitta rolled her eyes. "Alwilda! You know better than that. Father always yelled at us."

Alwilda stared at her sister defiantly. A lip quivered. Tears welled in her eyes, and a stifled sob tore from her throat.

"Now what's the matter?" Linitta demanded.

The smaller girl's face crumbled into tears. "I miss Mother and Father. I want to go back home."

Linitta dropped the firewood in her arms and cradled her sister to her. "I know, but we can't. You've got to be brave. Mother and Father have gone away, and they can't come back."

For several seconds, Alwilda sobbed against her sister's chest. "Here," Linitta said, handing the smaller girl a lace handkerchief. "Stop crying and wipe your nose. Uncle Bill doesn't like crybabies."

Alwilda scrubbed at her nose. "I am not a crybaby either."

"Then stop crying," Linitta replied. "Stop crying and help me carry this firewood back to the wagon."

Bill was sitting on Bumpo near the remuda when he spotted the girls struggling into camp loaded down with firewood. He watched curiously as Linitta deposited her wood near the fire, and then directed her sister to the possum belly.

With a click of his tongue, he walked Bumpo to the chuck wagon where the girls were busy loading firewood in the cowhide slung under the wagon.

"Glad to see you're giving Pancake a hand, girls," he said. Both looked around, surprised to see him.

He chuckled. "Don't let me stop you. Go ahead and fill the possum belly."

"Why do they call it a possum belly, Uncle Bill?" Alwilda asked. "Isn't that some kind of animal?" While she talked, Linitta finished loading the belly.

"You ever seen a possum, girl?"

Alwilda shook her head. "No, sir."

"Well, a possum's got a pouch, a bag in its belly." He pointed to his stomach. "That's where she carries her babies until they're old enough to take care of themselves. So we tie a cowhide under the wagon to carry firewood."

Linitta's eyes brightened. "And that's why you call it a possum belly, huh?"

Bill laughed. "That's right. Round here, there's plenty

of wood just for the pickin', but later, we'll hit stretches where you won't spot any firewood for days.''

"What do we do when we don't have no firewood?'' Alwilda asked.

"Well, then we'll use buffalo chips.''

"Buffalo chips? What's that?''

Millie had approached. Bill grinned sheepishly at her. "Buffalo chips? I reckon that's something I'll explain when the time gets here.''

Millie laughed. "Come on, girls. Let's help Mr. Pancake clean up.''

Bill cleared his throat. "We got an easy trail the next couple days. Ought to reach San Antone by then.'' An idea struck him. He hesitated, unsure if it was such a good idea. Why not? The girls seemed to be turning into good hands. "There's not much needin' my attention this afternoon. How'd you girls like a ride on Bumpo?''

Linitta jumped up and clapped her hands. She squealed. "Oh, yes, Uncle Bill. That would be wonderful.''

Alwilda frowned up at Millie. She wasn't any too certain she liked the idea of sitting on that big horse.

"Good,'' Bill said. "Once we get the herd strung out, I'll come back and pick you up. One at a time. If that's okay with Millie here,'' he added.

Linitta spun on the young woman. "Please, Millie. Please, Can I, huh? Can I?''

Millie laughed, and Bill thought the blush that colored her tawny cheeks was just about as pretty as the wild roses back along the Rio Grande.

"Yes, you can. But you have to behave yourself until then, you hear? Now, let's help Mr. Pancake clean up.''

Chapter Eight

The afternoon drive was strung out for a mile or so across the rolling savannas. From time to time, white-tailed deer, startled from their beds, bounced across the rolling meadows to the adjoining thicket of oak and paused, looking back over their shoulders at the slow-moving herd.

Midafternoon, Bill rode up to the Conestoga. Linitta bounced with excitement. "You all set?"

"Oh, yes, Uncle Bill. I'm ready." The wagon lumbered to a halt.

Bill did a double take when he got a good look at his niece and her dress. "What's this?"

Millie laughed. "We had to make do with what we had. This is her riding outfit." The rear hem of her dress had been pulled forward between her legs and snugged around her waist with a belt, neatly improvising a riding habit for a young woman.

"Well," Bill drawled, grinning at the jerry-rigged outfit. "If it works, can't argue with it." He pulled Bumpo up beside the wagon. "Hop on behind me. Just throw a leg over and grab hold of me."

With a grin broad as a river, Linitta slid on behind Bill.

"Now, watch your heels," Bill warned her. "Touch Bumpo in the flank, and he'll give us a ride we won't forget.'' He glanced at her feet, then smiled to himself. At ten, she hadn't hit her growing spurt. Her legs weren't long enough to dangle her feet near his flanks.

"Here we go.'' He clicked his tongue, and Bumpo eased away from the Conestoga and fell in with the herd.

Shorty and Alkali were riding point.

"Hiya, boss,'' Alkali called with a laugh. He nodded to Linitta. "Breaking in a new hand, huh?''

Linitta blushed and held tighter. For the next thirty minutes, they rode through the herd. Each of the cowpokes teased the excited girl, for she had become a favorite. There was not a man jack there for whom she had not poured coffee or fetched a second helping of grub. And they had all witnessed her helping Pancake around the camp.

Bill kept Bumpo in a slow walk so as not to jar Linitta too much. "How do you like it?'' he asked over his shoulder.

"I love it, Uncle Bill. I love it.'' Her voice was bubbling with excitement. "And I love the country here. It's so much fun.''

Her last words both surprised and disturbed him. He had taken it for granted that the girls would hate Texas. They should. The rigors and hardships aged women and horses faster than strychnine aged Injun whiskey.

No, Texas was no place for a woman, not ones like the girls, nor one like Millie. They needed to be back east, at least to New Orleans. There, the genteel behaviors of civilization allowed them to age with grace.

Bill forced a laugh. "Well, time to pick up your sister. Give her a ride.'' He deliberately chose not to respond to her remarks. After all, she was only ten. What did ten-year-olds know?

Alwilda refused a ride. At first, she agreed, but when it came to climbing on Bumpo, she backed out. "I'm scared. Bumpo will bite me."

Patiently Millie calmed her. "Pet him. He won't hurt you."

Stubbornly she shook her head.

Bill didn't try to change her mind, but he studied the eight-year-old while Millie spoke with her, comparing the obstinate child with her older sister. That one he wouldn't miss when they went back east. Linitta, well, she was a well-behaved kid, but even so, Bill would be glad when he put them on the stage for Boston.

"Maybe another time," Millie said, glancing up at Bill.

The rancher nodded and forced a grin. "Yeah. Later."

"Can I ride again tomorrow, Uncle Bill? Huh?" Linitta had loosened her belt and her dress had fallen back into place.

"We'll see. We'll see."

He turned Bumpo back to the herd. To his surprise, he found himself planning the next step in teaching his niece to ride.

Two days later, Bill bedded the herd just outside San Antonio. That night around the campfire, he spoke to Millie and the girls. "In the morning, I'm sending Pancake in to stock up on supplies. It's a far piece to Fort Griffin, and we can't bank on sufficient supplies there. If you ladies care to ride in with us, you're welcome. San Antone'll be the last fair-size town till we hit Dodge. Little place ahead called Buffalo Gap and then Fort Griffin. Not much at either."

The girls smothered Millie with pleas and promises.

She caved in. "All right, but you get to bed early, and no giggling, you hear?"

"Yes, ma'am," Alwilda said, leading the race to the Conestoga.

Bill grinned at Millie. "A little bribe, huh?"

She returned his smile. "With kids, you do it any way you can." She stared at the fire.

"I'm learning that," he said, leaning back on his saddle, cradling a hot tin of coffee in his hands, and trying to remember what a trail drive without women had been like.

"They're nice girls," she said. "It's a shame about their parents."

Neither spoke for several minutes. Bill dismissed the urge to tell her about his boyhood and his ongoing war with his brother. In the distance, a coyote yelped. Somehow, the plaintive cry was a source of comfort to Bill. "What are your plans when this is all over? Go back to Boston?"

Millie swirled her coffee and watched it thoughtfully. "I hope not." She paused, chewed on her lip, then looked directly into Bill's eyes. "Once I thought about settling down with a proper husband and family, but now, I'm not sure what I want. The storm. The river crossing. I . . . I think I'm beginning to see what you meant about Texas. Out here, you live on the edge. You can't afford mistakes. One thing this drive has helped me realize is that I don't want to live my life where I know what will happen tomorrow, and the day after, and the day after. So, when this is all over, maybe I'll go on to California, or even Oregon."

Bill had the distinct feeling Millie was daring him to argue with her. He couldn't pinpoint what she had said, or just how she said it to create that feeling, but create it she had. He sipped his coffee. "Sounds good to me," he replied, wondering if all women possessed the capability of confusing a man for no reason at all.

"You don't think I'm being foolish? Or harebrained?"

"Nope." Bill shrugged. "Man or woman, a body has to do what he wants. If California or Oregon is what calls a man, he has to go. Otherwise, he'd always be wonderin'."

The focus in Millie's eyes lost its edge as her gaze fell on the fire. "Like, what's on the other side of the hill? Is that what you mean?"

Bill pondered the question a few moments, then nodded. "Yep. I reckon it is. Restless feet. Some folks got them, and I don't suppose there's nothing to satisfy the itch than to see just what's over the next rise. That being the case, I couldn't blame a feller."

"Me neither," Millie whispered, more to the fire than Bill. "Me neither."

Standing behind the seat of the chuck wagon, Linitta and Alwilda bounced up and down with excitement as they rolled into view of San Antonio, a bustling village straddling the San Antonio River.

"Is it true what Alkali said, Millie? All of these people come from a foreign country?"

Millie, who was sitting next to Pancake, laughed. "Not exactly, Linitta. They come from Mexico, which is south and west of us a hundred or so miles. Isn't that right, Mr. Pancake?"

The crotchety old greasy belly hadn't said a word

since they'd pulled out of camp an hour earlier. He grunted. "I reckon."

Bill, who rode beside the wagon, grinned. One look at Pancake's frowning, irascible face told Bill he wasn't the only one having trouble adjusting to the girls. "Pancake's right, girls. Mexico is south of us, but the Mexicans settled this part of Texas more'n a hundred and fifty years ago with presidios and chapels and such. Then Americans began coming in about thirty or forty years back."

Linitta frowned. "You mean, this isn't the United States?"

"Sure it is. Sure it is. Texas is part of the United States now."

"But, if the Mexican people came here first, why isn't it theirs?"

Bill cut his eyes at Millie, who gave him a rueful smile and quickly looked away, pretending she had not heard Linitta's question.

"Well. Yeah, they was here first, but then other people, beginning with Stephen Austin, settled. He even brought in a sloughful of settlers. Then, about twenty-five, thirty years ago, the United States had a war with Mexico. We won." He made a sweeping gesture to the village. "And all of this belongs to the United States."

"Oh." Linitta grew thoughtful. "The United States just took it away from them, huh?"

"Not exactly." He started to continue, but he wasn't sure just what to say. He'd never dwelt on the war. On the right or wrong of it, not that there was anything wrong about avenging the Alamo and Goliad. All he had ever done, as most other Texans, was try to keep his ranch together.

Pancake tilted his head and shot a curious glance at Bill.

"When I was just a child," Linitta said, "I took a toy from Alwilda, and Father made me give it back. He said it wasn't right to take things that belonged to other people."

Bill pursed his lips. A sheen of sweat covered his forehead. He was trodding on unsteady ground. "Well, I reckon he was right . . . as far as it goes. You see . . . countries are different. They're real big, and they're made up of a whole bunch of people, and . . . well, they're different because of that."

"But how does that make it different, Uncle Bill, huh?"

"Well, it just does. That's one of those things that's hard for people to understand. And I reckon to a young lady like yourself, it does seem like a puzzle."

Pancake looked at him, squirted a stream of tobacco on the wagon tongue, and shook his head. Without saying a word, he turned back to his four-up.

A handful of gaudily dressed caballeros came racing out of the village, shouting and waving their sombreros over their heads. Immediately Linitta forgot her questioning and turned her full attention to the carefree young men, pointing after them as they swept past.

Bill breathed a sigh of relief. His answers had been only a shade more than incoherent. He grinned sheepishly at Millie, but she just arched an eyebrow and shook her head.

Bill led the way into the village down one of the many narrow dirt streets lined by flat-roofed, low-slung adobes. *Señoras* and *señoritas*, wearing bright shawls and sweeping skirts, hurried up and down the street, going about their daily chores. Millie and the girls were busy pointing out strange sights to each other and burying Pancake under a pile of questions.

The small group entered a large plaza, surrounded on four sides by bustling businesses of every imaginable description. Rickety *carretas,* small carts with large wooden wheels, filled the middle of the plaza, harnessed to large-boned oxen that stood woodenly in the hot sun, heads drooping, eyes closed.

Under a stand of cottonwoods, long wooden tables were heaped with fruits and vegetables for sale, produce harvested by the slender, brown-skinned Mexicans with flashing smiles and shining eyes.

An array of birds fluttered to the ground, pecking at discarded food. Small flocks of chickens clucked and cackled as they scratched their way around the plaza. Dogs of every color and size ran loose, chasing the chickens, playing with the laughing children, and dodging the angry merchants.

Bill led the way across the plaza, skirting the *carretas* loaded with firewood or cane or hay—or any of a hundred other products sought daily by the villagers. He stopped in front of a large adobe shop, El Toro Negro. "The Black Bull," he explained when Millie asked. "The owner, Luis Francisco Hernan Gaspar de Galvez, was once a toreador in Mexico City. Not one of the few good ones, but he made enough money to establish this business, the Black Bull."

"Can we go inside, Uncle Bill? Please?"

Bill nodded to Millie. "I've got some other business here in town. If Millie wants to go in with you, it's fine with me. Just don't interfere with Pancake. He's got to stock up on supplies. And if I'm not back here when you leave, listen to him. He's the boss. Understand?''

Both girls nodded emphatically. Alwilda spoke up. ''We understand, Uncle Bill. We understand.''

Bill hesitated. That was one the few times the younger girl had said anything that wasn't a whine or a complaint. It was a nice feeling, but he didn't figure it was a permanent change. She was just excited about the strange village around her.

''And don't forget what I told you to pick up, Pancake.''

The old cookie squinted up at him. ''Don't worry, Mr. Merritt. I won't forget.''

Chapter Nine

"Can I have another drink of water, Mister Pancake, please?"

Pancake looked over his shoulder at the red face of the smaller girl. She was breathing rapidly, and sweat glistened on her forehead. An unbidden grin broke the scowl on his wrinkled face. He reached under the seat and handed her the canteen. "I told you girls them chiles and beans was right hot, especially for a tenderfoot what never et none of them."

Linitta took the canteen from Alwilda. "Is all of their food that hot, Mr. Pancake?" She gulped three or four swallows. Then it was Millie's turn.

"You git used to it," he drawled. "Purty soon, you build up a stomach like rock, and nothin' bothers it."

Alwilda wiped the perspiration from her forehead. "I couldn't ever get used to it. My tongue still burns."

"Mine too."

Millie laughed. "And mine. But your food isn't that hot, Mr. Pancake."

Pancake chuckled. "Reckon not. I calmed it down some fer you ladies. Some of the boys complained, what from growing up on hot peppers and chiles. But ain't none of them that can stomach the hot peppers them Mex folks can."

"What kind of meat did they put in the beans? It was good. Was it beef?"

"Goat," he replied.

"Goat? Ugh." Alwilda made a face.

"But it was good," Millie exclaimed. "How did they make it so tasty, Mr. Pancake?"

"Well, the first thing they do is . . ."

And for the remainder of the ride back to the camp, Pancake answered their questions about Mexican dishes and ended up promising to teach them how to prepare some of his own specialties.

"Bill ain't here," Alkali said when the chuck wagon pulled up. "Wasn't he with you?"

Pancake looked over his backtrail. "Nope. He left us in the plaza. Said to come on back when we finished. I reckoned he'd be here, but that business of his must've took longer than he expected."

Millie and the girls climbed down.

Alkali said, "Well, he'll be along directly. You get ever'thing?"

"Yep." He fished among the packages for the special order Bill had told him to pick up. "And then some." He tossed the brown paper package down to Millie. "Bill said this was for the girls. I don't know what he's got on his mind, but this here's for them."

Both girls danced around Millie in delight. "A present, a present."

"What on earth?" Millie studied the package. She looked at the girls. "What kind of present could this be?"

"Open it," Pancake said. "Reckon that's the simplest way to find out."

"Open it, Millie. Please, open it," Alwilda shouted.

Millie shook her head. "It's your gift." She handed it to them. "You open it."

With a squeal of happiness, they grabbed the package and ripped the paper off. The smiles on their faces faded as they held up denim trousers and cotton shirts, just the size to fit each girl.

Puzzled, Linitta looked up at Pancake. "Uncle Bill told you to buy these for us?"

Pancake nodded and squirted a stream of tobacco juice on the ground. "Yep."

"Why?" Alwilda asked. "Girls don't wear boys' clothes. It isn't proper."

Millie looked down the road toward the village. A broad smile sprang to her lips. "I'll bet that's why," she said.

"What?" Linitta looked up at her.

"There. Down the road. There comes your Uncle Bill."

The girls ran around the rear of the wagon and slid to a halt, unable to believe their eyes.

Astride Bumpo, Bill Merritt was leading two small pinto ponies, a small saddle on each.

The girls looked at each other, whooped, tossed their new clothes to Millie, and broke for the approaching horses.

"Hey, there. Hold on," Alkali yelled. "You'll spook 'em."

Despite their excitement, the girls stopped.

Wearing a broad grin on his freckled face, Alkali explained. "Them little fellers are kinda skittish. This here is something new to them, just like it is to you. You go runnin' up like a couple wild Injuns, you'll scare them." He waved the girls back to the wagon. "Just wait here."

Dancing with excitement, the girls backed up to the

chuck wagon and watched with wide-eyed anticipation as Bill and the ponies drew nearer.

After what seemed like hours, he pulled up at the wagon and grinned down at the girls. He shoved his Stetson on the back of his head and drawled, "I ran across these two jugheaded animals back down the road. You know any little girls who might want them?"

The girls were so excited, they couldn't talk. All they could do was nod their heads.

Bill ran his eyes over their dress. "Well, you girls look right pretty in those little dresses and pinafore things. But dresses aren't made for riding." He looked across at Pancake. "You buy 'em what I asked?"

Millie held up the store-bought clothes. "These what you're talking about?"

The rawboned rancher eyed the clothes, then the girls. "Yep. Reckon a body's got to have the right kind of clothes if they want to ride a horse."

Alwilda and Linitta stared at each other, eyes wide in disbelief. After a couple seconds, the implication of his words hit them. As one, they leaped upon the wagon wheel, grabbed their store-bought clothes from Millie, and dashed for the Conestoga, peeling off pinafores and unbuttoning dresses while they ran.

Five minutes later, the girls were back, wearing their jeans and cotton shirts. Pump Harger had ridden up, and he and Alkali stood by the fire, sipping afternoon coffee and grinning at the excited girls. Pancake fussed around the chuck wagon, banging pots and pans, trying to pretend the whole affair was a waste of time, but his sidelong glances did not go unnoticed.

Bill and Millie stood by the two ponies, almost identical paints no more than four feet high at the withers. "Nip and Tuck. That's their names," said Bill. "Nip here has a black star here on his forehead. That's the only difference in the two.''

Alwilda stepped forward. ''Can I have him, Uncle Bill? Please?''

The amiable smile faded from his face. ''Well, now girls, I don't know. There's something we need to talk about first. And that's taking care of your animals.'' He pointed to the remuda. ''Out here, a horse is just about the most important friend a man can have. You got to look after him. Now, listen hard to what I'm going to tell you. First, I'm not going to give you the ponies.''

The girls' faces sagged. Alwilda's bottom lip quivered.

''I'm not going to give them to you, but what I'm going to do is loan them to you until I see you can take care of them and handle them. If I'm satisfied you're a good friend to these little fellers, then I'll give them to you. But you're going to have to be able to catch them and saddle them. On a drive like this, everyone's got to pull his own weight. Understand?''

''Yes, Uncle Bill,'' the girls replied in unison.

''Now, I asked Alkali and Pump to give me a hand with all this. They've punched cattle with me for years, and there's nobody who knows horses better'n them.'' Bill turned to Alkali. ''How about showing Alwilda what she needs to know about Nip here. Make her into a regular cowboy . . . cowgirl. Okay? And Pump, I'd be obliged if you'd do the same for Linitta.''

The two cowpokes tossed the last of their coffee on the fire. ''You bet, boss,'' Pump said. ''You bet.''

''And loop a strip of rawhide around them stirrups.''

''Yes, sir.''

While the two punchers helped the girls into the saddles and fit their toes under the rawhide tied around the stirrup, Bill squatted and poured two cups of coffee.

Millie sat on a log that had been rolled near the fire.

"That's a fine thing you did."

He glanced around. "What? Oh, the ponies. Naw. Selfish on my part. Figured it was the easiest way to keep them out of trouble. Two kids, nothing to do but sit around in a bone-jarring wagon. If that had been me bouncing around these last few weeks, I'd probably already have burned something down."

Millie laughed. "You don't sound much like that grumpy old man at the beginning of the drive."

"Well, you and the girls aren't much like those citified dudes who caused me those problems at the beginning of the drive."

She laughed again. He sipped his coffee, and a feeling of contentment washed over the lanky rancher.

Ramón pickup up the coffeepot. He poured himself a cup and held the pot out to Bill and Millie. "No, thanks," Bill said. "How were things while we were gone? Any problems?"

"No problems, boss." Ramón slid the pot back in the coals. "Spotted some Injuns off to the west, but they just kept on riding."

Bill rose to his feet. "How many?"

"Three." Ramón held up three fingers. "No more. They rode to the north. Too far to tell what tribe."

Millie's face grew somber. "Something wrong?"

"Huh? Oh, no, no. Nothing to worry about. Injuns. They were probably out hunting, or maybe visiting another tribe."

"Visiting another tribe? I thought . . . I mean, I'd always heard that Indian tribes didn't get along. That they fought each other all the time."

Bill snorted. "That's white man talk. Makes good reading for folks back east. Indians do fight. But, for the most part, they're like white people. Some tribes visit. Other tribes fight. But, like I said, for the most part, they're fair and honest men.'' He gestured to the sprawling countryside around them and added, with a touch of sarcasm, ''Out here, of course, you don't take a man's word that he's fair and honest. You do, you'll find yourself dead right fast.''

A shout from one of the girls interrupted them. Linitta was riding Tuck by herself, at a walk, but she was handling the reins. Pump glanced at Bill and nodded.

''Bill!'' Millie grabbed his arm. ''Alwilda. Look at Alwilda.''

The girl was trotting Nip.

''Should she be doing that so soon?''

Bill grinned. ''Relax. She's okay. Alkali wouldn't let her trot the pony if he didn't think she could handle him.''

They watched as the younger girl reined the pony through small and large circles. Bill compared the two girls. Linitta, though older and larger, bounced in the saddle, but Alwilda seemed to be flowing with the movement of the pony, her small body instinctively matching the rhythm of the horse.

''I don't know,'' Bill said, impressed. ''But that girl looks like she belongs on a horse.''

The next few days were uneventful. The herd plodded over the rolling savannas, crossing narrow streams and nooning in the shade of spreading oaks.

Both girls lived every minute of the day for their ponies, feeding, grooming, and caring for them as well as regularly oiling and rubbing their saddles. Within a week, Alwilda was racing Nip in circles around Linitta and Tuck, but the girls always remained within sight of the Conestoga.

"That little Alwilda's a natural, boss," Alkali said one evening as the punchers bedded down the herd. "She rides like she was born on a horse."

Bill agreed. It appeared both girls were turning into Westerners. Too bad it would end in a couple more months. Suddenly, the rancher realized his own thoughts and frowned. Too bad it would end in a couple more months? What was he thinking? Too bad? *Thank the Lord* was what he should be saying.

Linitta spotted the two men palavering and rode up to them. She presented a comical figure on horseback, wearing a slat bonnet and laced, high-top shoes. Bill made a mental note to outfit the girls with boots and hats at Abilene.

"Hello, Uncle Bill, Mr. Jones."

"How are you and Tuck doing?"

"Just wonderful, Uncle Bill. When are you going to let us help with the herd?"

Bill grinned at Alkali. "One of these days. You need to get real comfortable with that pony of yours."

"Uncle Bill?"

"Yeah?"

"Why can't Millie ride with us?"

The idea had never entered his mind. "I reckon she can if she wants to."

She cocked her head aside and frowned. "You don't care?"

"No. Why should I?"

Linitta grinned and wheeled Tuck around. "I'll go tell her."

"What was that all about?" Alkali asked, watching the cloud of dust billowing from the pony's hooves.

Bill sighed. "Beats me. What with three women

around, I run across puzzling things every day.''

The *segundo* chuckled. ''Know what you mean. I never figured a sprout could ask as many questions as that girl can. Smart kid too.''

''Yeah,'' Bill replied. ''They're both smart.''

''I can tell you this, they caught on right fast about them ponies. I swear if those animals don't follow the girls around like puppies.''

Bill chuckled. He had noticed the same thing. Maybe he could figure out some way to send the ponies back to Boston with the girls.

Ahead of the herd, Linitta pulled up beside the wagon. Bill could make out she was talking to someone, probably Millie. Seconds later, the ten-year-old raced back across the prairie toward the two men.

Along the way, Alwilda spotted her sister and pulled up beside her just as Linitta reined up in front of Bill. ''I told Millie, Uncle Bill. But she doesn't have a horse.''

The rawboned rancher shrugged. ''We got plenty in the remuda.''

Alkali cleared his throat and whispered under his breath. ''They all only half broke. I wouldn't trust no tenderfoot on any of them jugheads.''

His *segundo* was right. Not a solitary horse in the remuda would do, not without a considerable amount of time wasted in breaking one.

''Why don't you let her ride Bumpo, boss. We both seen how he lets her and the girls pet him.''

Bill opened his mouth to refuse. No one rode his horse, but then he hesitated. What could it hurt? She wouldn't be riding him everyday. Bill arched an eyebrow. ''I'll think on it.'' But, deep down, he knew he probably would let Millie ride Bumpo.

Chapter Ten

The days passed without incident. The strung-out herd averaged around twenty miles a day.

"Can't beat that, boss," Alkali drawled. "A couple more days, and we'll be at the Colorado."

The two cowboys were on the crest of a small hill overlooking the mile-long train of cattle. Bill Merritt removed his sweat-stained Stetson and studied it. "Reckon first thing I buy in Dodge is a new hat." He wiped the sweat from his face with his neckerchief and tugged his hat back on good and snug.

The bay gelding under him shifted its feet nervously. He patted the animal's neck. "Steady, fella."

"Makes a big difference without your own animal, huh, boss?"

Bill searched the point of the herd. There, a couple hundred yards to the side of the point riders were the three women, the girls on their frisky ponies, and Millie riding Bumpo.

"They're turning into fair riders, boss," Alkali said, studying Millie and the girls.

Bill growled. "I reckon they should. They're getting enough practice."

The testiness in his tone caught Alkali's attention. He grinned. "Well, what'd you sooner have, a girl causing stampedes, or one riding and mindin' her own business?''

Bill didn't reply for several seconds. Then he muttered, "Hope that jughead doesn't cause her any trouble."

Alkali grinned. "You know better'n that, boss. Old Bumpo, he ain't dumb. He knows when he's got it good."

Bill frowned. "What the blazes you talking about now?"

Alkali grew serious. "Why, Bumpo. He's a right smart animal." The redheaded *segundo* nodded to Bill. "Why should he carry a hundred and eighty pounds of smelly cowboy when he can haul around a tiny, sweet-smelling thing like Miss Millie?"

With a pained sigh, Bill rolled his eyes. "That's got to be about the dumbest thing you've ever said." But Bill had noticed how Bumpo had taken to Millie. And a part of him was a little jealous though he would not admit it. He was glad, he told himself, that he had a horse like Bumpo for her, one that would keep her out of trouble, and out of his hair so he could handle the cattle drive.

"I don't know, boss. There's something almost magical-like about them women and Bumpo. You got to admit, other than you, they're the only jaspers he's ever tolerated."

Bill clicked his tongue and started the bay down the hill. "Come on," he said with a growl. "We got work to do." In the back of his mind, he decided to find Millie a horse of her own.

With a chuckle, Alkali joined him. "Yes, sir. Right behind you."

* * *

That night, just after the first shift of nighthawkers rode out to the herd, a shout came from the darkness beyond the campfire. "Hello, the fire. I'm a friend. Can I come in?"

Instantly, every cowboy laid his hand on the butt of his six-gun. Bill gestured for Millie and the girls to move closer to the Conestoga. "Come on in," he called back.

He sensed someone at his back. He glanced around. Alwilda was edging forward, her neck craned so she could peer into the darkness. "I said get back. You hear?"

At Bill's sharp words, Millie hurried forward and seized the girl's hand and pulled her back to the wagon.

From the darkness came the grunt of horses and the thump of hooves against the hard soil. Two men rode into the firelight, arms extended to their sides. One had a thick black beard and wore a broad-brimmed hat with a sugarloaf crown. "Howdy." He indicated his companion. "This here's my *segundo*, Rufus Buchanan. I'm Athol Rogers. We're pushing beeves north for Earl Simmons, down in Webb County."

Bill shot a look at Alkali, who nodded and disappeared into the night. "Light and squat. Coffee's on. I'm Bill Merritt out of Hidalgo County. We heard about you old boys."

"Obliged," Rogers drawled, climbing down and reaching for the coffee. With a rock-steady hand, he filled his cup and that of his *segundo*. They remained standing. "Can't stay. Our herd's beyond the Colorado. Two thousand head. We're looking for strays. Circle Cross is the road brand. Seen any in yours?"

Rising to his feet, Bill looked around at his men. "Any you boys spotted a Circle Cross?"

"Not me," Shorty Wilson replied. Several other punchers shook their heads.

"Be glad to cut the herd in the morning if you got a mind to spend the night."

Rogers scratched his beard. "Reckon not. Truth is, I don't suspect we'll find them. If I was you, Mr. Merritt, I'd make a point not to bed down in the Colorado bottoms."

Alkali came back into the firelight and nodded at Bill who relaxed somewhat. "Why's that, Mr. Rogers?"

"Range cattle. Couple nights back, around midnight, range cattle hit our herd. Faster'n you can say Jack Robinson, they scattered the herd to every direction on the compass. Now, it might be that wolves spooked the range cattle, but I reckon if it was wolves, it was the human kind." He drained his coffee and headed for the chuck wagon, where he washed and dried his cup while he spoke. "We got them rounded up next day, but picked up a few hundred head of local stock. Spent today cutting them. We're around five hundred head short. That's just about all our profit."

"You pushing on?"

Rogers shook his head. "Can't say for sure. Hate to put you in a bind like this. If we find more of our stock tomorrow, we'll move on out. If not, then we'll hang around till we find them or figure they's done run off to Abilene. We've already lost a couple weeks. I hate to lose more time."

Bill considered the situation that had been dumped in his lap. "Yep, you got us in a bind, but I can truly see the fix you're in."

''You're welcome to move ahead of us if we don't find our cattle.'' He climbed into his saddle. ''You find any Circle Crosses in your herd, Mr. Simmons would appreciate you settling up with him when it's convenient.''

''Happy to, Mr. Rogers.'' Bill patted his six-gun. ''And thanks for the warning.''

Rogers touched his fingers to the brim of his hat, and the drovers disappeared into the night.

''I reckon he's done given us something to think on, huh, boss?''

Bill stared into the darkness after the two riders. ''Yep. I figure he has done just that.'' After several moments, the rawboned rancher squatted and poured himself another cup of coffee.

The camp grew quiet. Cowboys pulled their tarps back over them and snuggled down for a few hour's sleep. Millie and the girls retired to the Conestoga. Within ten minutes, only Bill and Alkali remained by the fire.

Bill spoke in a whisper. ''I've heard talk that west of here harbors some of the worst rustlers in the state. Never gave it much thought, but now, I reckon it's time to consider it.''

''Suppose you're right, boss. What with the Circle Crosses only a couple days ahead, I figure we ought to rest up here a few days. I ain't anxious to mix our three thousand up with theirs.''

''Maybe. Maybe not. To tell the truth, I don't particularly cotton to following the Circle Crosses all the way to Dodge.'' He studied the situation for several minutes. ''The flood bottoms at the crossing are about five miles on either side. You figure we can make it from one side to the other in one day?''

Alkali grimaced. "That's ten miles of bottoms plus the ford. We'd be pushing it mighty hard, boss."

"What if we pushed a straight line of cattle across the river, not break it into blocks? Shorty and Catman have some good water horses. They could handle the down-river side."

Without waiting for Alkali to reply, Bill nodded sharply. "That's exactly what we're going to do, except, we'll have to push on past the Circle Crosses. Another five miles."

"That'll take us into a night drive, boss."

Bill cut his eyes at Alkali and grinned. "That's why these old boys of ours are getting paid the princely sum of thirty dollars a month, right?"

All Alkali could do was shake his head.

Bill added, "We're not waiting on the Circle Crosses to move out. We'll push through. I don't wish bad luck on any hombre, but we're not going to be hurt by their ill wind."

"What if they've moved out?"

"Well, I reckon then we'll be forced to rest up a few days. Maybe a week. I don't cotton trailing them. We do and all we'll push into Dodge will be skin and bones."

Word spread quickly through the camp. The anticipation of such a concentrated effort sharpened the senses of the cowpunchers, whetted their enthusiasm. For weeks the punchers had ridden side by side with boredom, sharing a bedroll monotony, but now they had some excitement coming their way.

They were going to hit the river with a mile-long line of cattle and drive it across without stopping. For one of the few times on the drive, they wouldn't be slouching in the saddle of a pony moseying along at the pace of a one-legged cowpoke with a broken crutch. They would be standing high in the stirrups and screaming at the top of their lungs.

Two hours before sunrise, the wagons, accompanied by Shorty Wilson and Catman Johns, moved out, followed by a line of milling cows. Creatures of habit, the cattle sensed they were moving out too early. Several tried to turn back, but the flankers were there to turn the bawling cattle back into the line.

The moonlight illumined the trampled trail, which was a couple hundred feet wide where it dropped into the bottom and cut through the tangled thickets and giant oaks.

Within minutes, the wagons were out of sight.

Bill rode up beside Alkali. "Keep your eyes peeled."

"Don't worry, boss. We got flankers out wide. Any stray dogies try to come in, we'll drive 'em back."

The rawboned rancher sat back in his saddle and studied the thick bottoms around them. A hundred riders could be hiding within a hundred feet. He touched the butt of his .45 and smiled grimly as he glanced at his own punchers, a dozen cowmen who had not the least compunction to fight and scratch for their cows. Any rustlers out there, they'd sure be in for a surprise.

Without incident, the herd reached the Colorado River by midmorning and plunged into the swift current. When the cows hit the far shore, Bill allowed them to spread through the bottom, grazing while the tail end of the herd was pushed across.

The sun had peaked, then begun its journey to the west by the time the last dogie crossed the river. Without hesitation, the point riders pushed out the lead steers, heading out of the bottom.

Shorty Wilson came riding up. "Simmons's herd is just ahead, boss. Pancake moved on. Said he'd find a spot to bed the herd."

Bill wheeled Bumpo around and barked his orders. "Hold 'em in tight, boys. When we hit the Circle Crosses, swing wide."

The Circle Crosses were grazing on the savanna next to the bottom. The Bar Slash point men nudged the lead steers out to the right, keeping several hundred yards between the herds.

Once the herd passed the Circle Crosses, Bill rode ahead. An hour later, he spotted the wagons in the evening shade of giant oaks on a bluff overlooking the river. He grinned as he quickly scanned the area.

Pancake had selected the perfect spot, a mile or so off the main trail just in case the Circle Crosses decided to stampede. Beyond the wagons, the river made a large bend, an ideal holding pen for the herd. He rode in. Pancake was busy building the fire for the evening meal. Ramón stood on the edge of the bluff overlooking the river.

Bill looked around for Millie and the girls, but they were nowhere to be seen. Suddenly, shouts from the river caught his attention. He slammed his heels into Bumpo's flanks and raced to the river.

He pulled up beside Ramón at the edge of the dropoff and stared unbelievingly at the scene thirty feet below.

A sandbar had formed along the inside bend of the river, building a small pool between the bar and the shore. Linitta and Alwilda, wearing white shifts, were frolicking in the water while Millie watched from the river's edge.

Alwilda laughed, and her tiny voice echoed across the river. Bill grinned, at the same time instinctively studying the thick undergrowth lining the far bank. If there were any stray Indians or owlhoots around, the girls' laughter would draw them. But he saw nothing.

He reined Bumpo around and eased the roan stallion down the slope. Linitta waved when she spotted him.

Millie looked up at him, a broad smile on her lips. She nodded to the girls. "Why don't you join in?"

Bill chuckled and dismounted. His eyes never stopped moving, surveying the broad, swirling river to the next bend, then moving up the steep bank to the undergrowth on the bank and back along the edge to the girls. "Reckon it wouldn't hurt, but maybe another time."

Ears perked forward, Bumpo stood on the bank, staring at the splashing girls.

The smile on Millie's face faded. "You see something?"

"Huh? Oh, no, but out here, a jasper can't be too careful." He hesitated and glanced up the bluff behind them for Ramón, but the young caballero had disappeared. At least, Bill told himself, Millie hadn't taken the girls away from camp without someone looking out for them.

"I know," she replied. She pointed to the top of the bluff. "That's why I asked Ramón to . . . oh, he's gone. But he *was* there, watching us," she added defensively.

Bill nodded. "I saw him. That was smart. But . . . thing is, sometimes one hombre just can't do it. It's always the best out here to stay together."

A light blush colored her cheeks, but she set her jaw

and looked the tall rancher in the eyes. "Why do I always feel I can't do anything right around you?"

Her question took him by surprise. For a fleeting moment, he was torn between the truth and the western tenet of protecting women from harm and embarrassment. But he had grown from a yonker to manhood in the West; the creed was too strong to break. "That's not it. It just takes some time. You . . . all three of you are doing just fine. Why, even Pancake has paid you a few compliments." The last statement was a bald-faced lie. Pancake never complimented anyone, but Bill couldn't see the harm in a white lie. "Like I said though, I'd rest easier if you were to stay within sight of the wagon."

The girls had continued splashing and laughing, and were presently involved in an enthusiastic water fight. Without warning, Bumpo waded into the pool and slapped the water with his front foot.

The water fight ceased immediately. Both girls stared up at the roan stallion in surprise. Bill and Millie were in shock. What was wrong with that jughead?

Bumpo stood motionless, ears forward, his large eyes on the girls, both of whom stood frozen. Then Bumpo slapped the water again.

Alwilda dropped to her knees and splashed water at the strawberry-colored animal. No sooner had the water sprayed Bumpo than he squealed and jumped back. He dashed in a circle and skidded to a halt in front of the girls.

The peculiar antics of the horse rendered Bill and Millie speechless. In the past, Bill had been witness to some of the quirky behavior of the stallion, but nothing like he was now seeing.

Bumpo splashed again, then shot in a circle, almost

like a playful dog chasing its tail. Mud and water sprayed from his flying hooves, splattering Bill and Millie and coating the girls with a layer of mud.

The girls screamed with delight as the red stallion dashed around in several more dizzying circles before skidding to a halt beside them in the ankle-deep water.

Alwilda laid her hand on Bumpo's pastern.

Bill hesitated, fearful his voice might startle the stallion and injure the girl. Linitta came to his rescue. She reached for the reins and tugged them loose from the saddle horn.

Bumpo stood docile as a lamb, staring down at her with his large, brown eyes. Bill stepped forward.

"I've never seen anything like that," Millie whispered.

With a rueful grin, the rawboned rancher chuckled and took the reins from Linitta. "Me neither, but nothing that jughead does surprises me. Nothing."

He looked down at the girls and shook his head. They were covered with mud from head to toe. "Best you girls clean up and head on back to the wagon." He glanced at the orange sky in the west and nodded at Millie who was also splattered with mud. "You got a few specks on you too."

She arched an eyebrow. "Look who's talking. You need a bath as much as we do."

He brushed at the mud on his red shirt and stuck a foot in the stirrup. "Maybe, but I got work to do. We'll be bringing the herd in after dark." He swung into the saddle, which, the girth loosened by Bumpo's madcap antics, immediately slipped, dumping Bill headlong into the ankle-deep water.

Chapter Eleven

Pancake, a taciturn and somber hombre by nature, choked on his tobacco when Bill rode up, soaking wet and mud-splattered. A grin cracked the old man's wrinkled face, but Bill's sharp glance warned him that silence was the wiser choice at the moment.

Without a word, the rancher paused at the side of the chuck wagon and fished in his soogan for a fresh shirt. He stuffed it in his saddlebags and rode upriver.

Later, he returned, his boots and denims still wet, but wearing a clean plaid shirt. Suppressing their laughter, Millie and the girls watched from the Conestoga and Pancake from under his eyebrows as Bill draped his faded red shirt over a low-hanging limb. Then, his back ramrod straight, he rode out to meet the herd without a glance at the cook or the girls while his red shirt swung in the breeze.

Before the herd moved out the next morning, Bill Merritt went to retrieve his shirt, but it was missing from the limb on which he had hung it the evening before. He shrugged, figuring Pancake had picked it up.

With a click of his tongue, he sent the black gelding he was forking to the point. He left Bumpo in the remuda, for Millie and the girls had planned to ride that morning.

Two hours into the drive, Bill and Alkali were astride their ponies on the crest of a small hill when Millie and the girls rode past and waved. Alkali grinned at Bill. "Miss Millie and them girls is turning in to right good riders. 'Course, the girls was fussing about the rawhide around the stirrup."

Bill looked down at the black gelding he was riding. "Yeah," he muttered. He was going to have to get Millie a pony of her own. He felt comfortable only with Bumpo. Any other cayuse made him spooky, not because he couldn't handle the animal, but because he didn't have the faith and trust in it as he did his big red stallion.

He pulled the black around and headed for the flank. "Stop jabbering and let's get to work."

With a grin, Alkali followed.

Later, the rancher and his *segundo* were riding flank when a handful of riders topped a hill to the east.

Alkali dropped his right hand to his thigh, inches from the butt of his six-gun. "What do you think, boss?"

"Can't tell." Bill studied the approaching riders warily. He counted four.

From the corner of his eyes, he picked up a blur moving into focus. Millie and the girls were riding in from the point, their attention turned to the oncoming riders also.

Motioning Millie and the girls to stay behind, Bill and Alkali rode out to meet the riders. "Howdy." Bill nodded.

The four riders were hardcases, rugged, unshaven, with weeks of dirt ground into their duds. The hombre in front grunted. The three jaspers behind him looked like coiled snakes. "We're looking for range stock in passing herds. Ever'time a herd pushes through, folks around here lose stock.'' The man's black eyes traveled to Millie and the girls, then snapped back to Bill and Alkali.

''Be happy to oblige,'' Bill replied. ''Though I don't reckon you'll find any. My *segundo* here keeps his eyes peeled for stock that don't belong.''

The first hombre snorted. ''Well, I seen *segundos* what looked the other way too.''

Alkali bristled. ''Mister, I think maybe you need to explain yourself a mite. You mean what I think you meant, then—''

Bill rode between the two men, making sure that Millie and the girls were to one side. ''Back off, Alkali.'' He turned to the hardcase. ''You accuse one of my boys, mister, you're accusing me.''

The hardcase tried to hold Bill's eyes, but failed. ''Wasn't talking about you boys. It's others.''

That was as much an apology as Bill was about to get, and he recognized the fact. ''Then let's get on to business. Alkali, circle the stock. Put a man with each of these boys and let 'em cut the herd. What brand you looking for?''

''Several.'' He looked away quickly. ''I'll know 'em when I see 'em.''

Bill studied him. The man's story didn't ring true. ''You got credentials, I suppose.''

The question took the man by surprise. He shot a glance at his three sidekicks. They looked away uncomfortably. He mustered his bravado. ''Me and my boys do this all the time for the locals.''

''That's not what I asked, mister. I asked to see papers that the locals signed that gives you the right to cut herds for their brands. Now, you either got them, or you don't.''

Alkali eased his pony aside for a clear shot in case gunplay started. He glanced at Millie and the girls. They were staring wide-eyed at the scene before them. He cursed to himself, wishing the women were farther away.

The muscles in his jaw twitching like a jarful of snakes, the hardcase glared at Bill. Long seconds passed. Finally, Bill grew tired of waiting. He eased the black backward a few steps. ''You boys come back with proper credentials, I'll oblige you, but the way it appears to me, you're just out and out rustling cattle the easy way.''

''Why you . . .'' The hardcase reached for his six-gun.

Alkali's hand was a blur. Before the owlhoot had cleared leather, Alkali had drawn down on him. ''Just hold it, mister. Unless you figure your skin's tougher'n a .45 slug.''

The rustler's bluster crumbled. He dropped his six-gun back into its holster and yanked his hand away. ''I don't want no shooting. That ain't why we come.''

A crooked grin played over Bill's lips. ''Well, at least you're smart. Stay smart and leave us alone.''

The hardcase glanced at Millie and the girls. Beneath the grime on his face, his cheeks colored. ''Maybe we ain't smart,'' he shot back. ''You ever think about that?''

Bill recognized the attempt to save face in front of the women. Another reason not to have women on the drive. He held his temper. ''Nope. I never thought about that. To be honest, I try not to think about hombres I have to bury along the trail.''

The outlaw's eyes narrowed. His body tensed.

Millie gasped.

Her muted gasp broke the tension. The outlaw backed away. "You ain't seen the last of me. I'll come back with enough boys to cut your herd to the bone."

"You do that. But you'd better come shooting if you don't have any paperwork."

He glared at Bill, then whipped his pony around and raked at the animal with his jangling spurs.

Alkali eased up beside Bill. "What do you think, boss? Double the guards?"

Bill tore his eyes from the retreating outlaws and glared at the women, who had no idea just how much danger they had been in. "Yeah. I reckon."

Millie and the girls approached, still goggle-eyed over the scene that had been played out before them. Bill pointed at the wagon. "Get them horses back to the wagon and stay there. You could've got yourselves killed. That's all women are good for out here."

His biting words slapped Millie across her cheeks, startling her. Her ears burned, and her reply stuck in her throat. She wheeled Bumpo around. "Come on, girls. Let's do what Mr. Merritt orders. Let's get back to the wagon."

Alkali pulled up beside Bill and clicked his tongue. "Know how you feel. Them women being so close spooked me too, but you was still kinda rough on her, wasn't you, boss?"

Bill kept his eyes on the women. "Maybe. You know as well as me, Alkali. Out here, there ain't no second chances. I got to admit, I'm no hand with kids . . . or women, for that matter. But I don't hanker to have them along the way either. I'm wishing now I'd not gone into this deal. I'd be content with half a ranch and those three back in Boston all safe and snug." He glanced after the outlaws. "Now, with what we got facing us, I . . ." He shrugged. "I'm not looking forward to it."

"I reckon I know what you mean, boss, but it's too late to worry about it now."

With a long sigh, Bill slumped in his saddle. The weight of the world pressed down on his broad shoulders. "Sure is, Alkali. Sure is."

That evening, a band of riders came in from the north, appearing from the thickets of shin oak as if by magic.

"They got back mighty fast," Alkali muttered, shucking his six-gun and spinning the cylinder.

Bill stood in his stirrups and squinted into the growing dusk. "Don't think so. The old boy in the lead sits his saddle different than those jaspers this morning. Let's go see," he added, kicking his horse toward the oncoming riders.

The band was a patrol of Texas Rangers, heading down to the Colorado and San Saba County beyond. "A little Comanche scare," said Sergeant Sam Cobb, punctuating his explanation with a stream of tobacco juice, the residual of which had stained his gray beard brown.

"We coulda used you this morning," Alkali said, who went on to tell the patrol about the rustlers.

Sam Cobb's eyes lit up. "Well, now, Mr. Merritt. If you got the means to put us up for the night, we'd be right pleased to straighten this mess out. We been hearing about these boys from other herds pushing through Abilene, but they been like the will-o'-the-wisp, vanishing just when we thought we had them. This could be our first chance to lay our hands on them."

Bill looked at the Rangers, hard, bearded men willing to walk into Hell and take on Old Scratch himself. He grinned, a weight suddenly lifted from his shoulders. "Cookie'll be right pleased to put on extra beans and coffee, Mr. Cobb."

That evening around the campfire, they laid their plans. Come morning, the Rangers would ride east and stay out of sight of the herd back in the timber. When the rustlers returned, Bill was to send word. Shorty Wilson grinned. "Reckon that'll take care of them rustlers," he said. "With thirteen of us and twelve Rangers, them fellers don't have a chance."

One of the Rangers rose to his full six-foot eight, stretched his arms, and said, "Don't know about you old boys, but I'm hittin' the sack. Want to rest up for our little Texas breakdown in the morning."

Bill studied the Texas Rangers; they were tall, rugged, somber men, with eyes that burned holes in a jasper, and steady hands equally skilled with a six-gun or a bowie knife. Yep, these were the no-nonsense kind of Texans who shaped the state, and the world. With the exception of Alkali and Catman, his own boys were young, just learning to shave, and vastly inexperienced. Game boys, but they couldn't take one step in the Rangers' boots.

Once or twice throughout the evening, Bill spotted one of the girls glancing from the pucker hole in the Conestoga. Millie never put in an appearance.

Long after Pancake banked the fire, Bill lay awake staring at the darkened Conestoga, cursing himself for being so sharp with Millie and the girls that morning. They were greenhorns, unfamiliar with the danger that hid behind every mesquite, every oak, every boulder, not to be blamed for what they didn't know, but if gunplay had broken out, all three could be lying dead back on the prairie.

Yet he couldn't confine them to the wagon for the rest of the trip. And even then, the unexpected could happen. The lanky rancher laced his fingers behind his head and looked up at the starry sky, tracing the familiar shape of the Big Dipper and wondering at the millions of tiny diamonds that made up the Milky Way. How cool and peaceful they appeared.

Just before he slipped into a light slumber, he wondered if somewhere up there, on some other planet, a cowboy was looking down at him, asking the same questions he was asking.

Next morning, while the Rangers bustled about readying their gear, Bill ordered Pancake to skip the nooning. ''Just push on and find us a good spot for tonight.''

Then he stopped by the Conestoga and told Millie to remain in the wagon. She nodded, but not before he caught the flicker of hurt in her eyes. He shook his head. ''Look. It's not because of yesterday. Yesterday, well, I . . .''

He hesitated, seeing the disbelief on her face. He explained. ''The truth is, we expect the rustlers back today. Sam and his Rangers are going to hit them when they come in. That's why I want you to stay in the wagon. You'll be out of danger.''

A faint smile replaced the hurt on her face. She nodded. ''Whatever you say.''

Bill hesitated, wanting to say more, to apologize, but all he could do was nod and stomp away.

The Rangers rode out minutes later under cover of darkness. ''Remember,'' Sam Cobb said, ''we'll be watching from just inside the timber, but just to be safe, send a rider flying as soon as you spot them owlhoots.''

Midmorning, Bill and Alkali spotted a cloud of dust a few miles behind the herd. ''Reckon it's dance time, boss,'' drawled the redheaded *segundo*. He shucked his six-gun and checked the cylinder.

Bill waved to Pump Harger, who whipped his pony around and hightailed it for the Rangers. ''Looks that way.''

Shorty Wilson headed for the point, planning on tightening the herd.

A quarter of a mile ahead, thick stands of shin oak and live oak jutted into the savanna from either side, forming a bottleneck. ''There's where we'll pull up,'' Bill said, turning in his saddle and studying the growing cloud of dust.

Alkali grinned at his boss's deviousness. ''Good idea,'' he replied. ''Be right nice, resting in the shade.''

Bill gave him a crooked grin. ''I don't reckon we'll get much resting done, do you?''

''Can't tell, boss. Can't tell.''

Behind them, the dust grew thicker. Soon, dark figures emerged from the cloud, heading straight for the herd, which was beginning to mill about just beyond the timber.

Bill glanced to the east, but spotted no sign of the Rangers. He slipped the rawhide loop off the hammer of his .45. All he could do now was wait.

Chapter Twelve

Bill and Alkali remained on their horses in the shade of the live oaks. Swede and Shorty rode up beside them.

Swede counted the oncoming riders. "I see fourteen. You t'ink t'ey got enough 'elp?"

Bill chuckled. "That's only about three to one. Shouldn't be no trouble for you boys." He wiped his sweaty palms on his denims.

The three hands laughed, but it was a nervous laugh.

The approaching riders spread out side to side in a skirmish line, fourteen hardcases ready to slap leather at the slightest provocation.

His eyes on the rustlers, Bill spoke softly to his men. "Now, boys, we're not here to see who can get himself killed first. We're here to drive cattle to Dodge. That's first. So don't go get yourself into a scrape. They got the numbers on us this time."

The riders pulled up. The galoot in front grinned, revealing a mouthful of rotting teeth. "I told you we'd be back."

Bill nodded. "Can't say I'm happy to see you, but I notice you brought more of your own sneaky kind with you."

The leer on the hardcase's lips faded. His voice was a hiss. "I told you I'd be back, and now I'm going to cut you so deep, you'll be lucky to get out of here with half your road brand.''

A few chuckles sounded from his men.

He sneered. "Okay, boys, start cutting.''

The sudden thunder of hooves caused the outlaws to jerk around. At the same time, Bill and his boys slapped leather. "Take it easy, boys,'' he barked. "You got visitors coming.''

The outlaws hesitated, frantically searching for a way out, but they had the herd on one side, four armed cowpokes on a second, and a dozen hard-riding men on the other two. The leader wheeled about and faced Bill. "You tricked me, you—''

"You tricked yourself when you turned bad, mister. Don't try to put the blame nowhere else. And don't try for that hogleg. I'm not anxious to stampede my cattle and run the tallow off them, but I'd just as soon blow your greasy head clean off without a second thought, and then chase my stock down.''

The outlaws milled about, looking for orders from their leader, but he was staring down the muzzle of a .45, and he didn't have any orders to give.

"Well, well, well,'' Sergeant Sam Cobb drawled as he pulled up. He pointed the muzzle of his .45 at the hardcase. "If it ain't Waco Brown. I think I got me some papers on you, Waco.''

By now, the Rangers had the outlaws surrounded.

Sam looked over the other owlhoots. He arched an eyebrow. "Well, now, ain't that No-Thumb Wallace back there? And ain't it a whopper of a surprise that I got papers on you. In fact, we probably got papers on most of you old boys here.'' He motioned to Waco's gun belt. "First thing you fellers do is drop them belts and rifles."

After the belts hit the ground, Sam Cobb nodded to one of his men. "Alvin, do me the favor of leading this miserable passel of owlhoots to one side so we can let Mr. Merritt and his boys move on out. By the way, Mr. Merritt, I'd be much obliged if you'd load them belts in your wagon. I'll take 'em off your hands when you reach Abilene." He nodded to the downcast outlaws. "You can see, I ain't got no room to haul that kinda load. 'Sides, if there ain't no guns around, these hombres can't get their hands on them. I reckon you could say I was doing them a favor by preventin' them getting shot full of holes."

Waco Brown snarled at Bill. "You think you done something smart? Well, you didn't. I'll be back, and I'll make you pay for this."

Cobb cracked the outlaw leader alongside the head with the muzzle of his six-gun. "Shut up, Waco. You ain't goin' to bother nobody no more. I'm going to enjoy watching you stretch a rope."

The sullen, angry expressions on the outlaws' faces vanished, replaced by wide-eyed fear and shaky voices. One young galoot whined to Sam Cobb, "Please, mister. I ain't done nothing. I just joined up with these boys this morning. There ain't no papers out on me."

Cobb looked the boy over. "Well, now, son. That may be, but even if I don't have papers on you, I'm taking you in to protect you against yourself. Any jasper with the poor judgment you've demonstrated in your choice of friends needs to be locked up for his own good." He gestured with the muzzle of his .45. "Now, git your carcass over with them others."

The Ranger grinned at Bill and holstered his hogleg. "Darn shame the young bucks get caught up like they do. Maybe some time in the hoosegow will knock some sense into his skull. But, anyways, Mr. Merritt, I appreciate your help. Snaking a lasso on these old boys will cut down on some of the outlawry hereabouts."

Bill chuckled and motioned to Swede. "Git a pony from the remuda and haul this gear to the wagons. Shorty, get on back to the point and get them dogies moving."

With a grin, both cowpokes wheeled their animals about.

That evening, their hurt feelings from the day before forgotten, the girls sat around the campfire listening in rapt attention to the events surrounding the capturing of the rustlers.

Alkali was telling the story, embellishing here and there until a jasper would have guessed the confrontation was a give-no-quarter, take-no-quarter shootout surpassing the Battle of Bull Run.

"Is that true, Uncle Bill, huh?" Linitta asked, her eyes wide in wonder.

The lanky rancher shook his head. "Naw, don't listen to that redheaded bag of air, Linitta. He's been known to tell some stretchers before, and this one looks like it's going to be one of his best."

The cowhands laughed, and Bill reached for the coffee.

Alwilda jumped up. "I'll get it, Uncle Bill," she exclaimed, stumbling forward. Her foot kicked the bottom of the pot, sending coals flying and hot coffee spraying.

"What the . . ." Bill jumped back, but the coals and

coffee caught him, first covering him with soot, then washing it down with coffee, which resulted in covering him with a thick, black sheen of mud.

The small girl froze, her clenched fists pressing into her lips. Her eyes were wider than tin plates.

Bill Merritt stood frozen, a sodden cowpoke dripping with coffee. He glared at the child.

Several cowhands ducked their heads, stifling their own laughter. Alkali bit his lips in an effort to hold back his laughter. His face turned redder than the coals scattered around the camp. Suddenly, the laughter fled his face. He spotted a tendril of smoke drifting upward from the crown of Bill's hat.

Before he could warn his boss, Bill shouted, yanked his hat off, and began pounding his head, trying to knock away the coal that had burned through his sombrero.

The cowhands had struggled mightily to contain their laughter, but Bill's newest antics ripped away their constraint, and the camp roared with glee.

Alwilda stood frozen, staring in horror at her lanky uncle, fearing his wrath. While Bill was bouncing around the fire like a wild Indian, trying to douse the fire in his hair, Millie hurried the frightened girl back to the Conestoga. Out of sight, out of mind, she told herself, barely able to contain her own mirth.

By the time the rawboned rancher had rid his hair of the burning coal and turned back to the fire, everyone had hastily rolled into their soogans and turned their faces to the darkness outside the camp. Even Alkali had disappeared. Bill heard his *segundo*'s voice cracking with amusement from the darkness as Alkali gathered a pony for the nighthawk shift.

"Blast that man," he muttered, stomping over to the

chuck wagon. He dipped water from the barrel and poured it over his head, trying to wash away some of the sticky grime. They were still two days from the Brazos and a bath.

Forty miles to the north, in a dry gulch that opened onto the Brazos, four Kiowa camped around a small fire. Behind them in a rope corral were twenty-four sleek Indian ponies, the price Bill had jokingly set for the sale of Millicent Deavers.

The next morning, a dozen unnaturally silent cowpokes wolfed down sourdough bullets and redeye gravy. Faint grins played over their faces, and they threw sidelong glances at their boss and each other, but not a word was spoken.

When Bill left for the remuda, Ramón slipped breakfast through the pucker hole to Millie and the girls, all of whom remained inside the Conestoga until the day's drive began.

The drive began earlier than usual, and Bill pushed the herd hard—too hard, Alkali claimed. "What's the hurry, boss? We're making good time."

Bill and Alkali sat on their ponies overlooking the flank of the herd. Dust billowed up around them. The rancher nodded in the general direction of his cowhands. "They're just sitting around getting fat and lazy. They need to get out there and earn their keep."

Alkali snorted. "Hey, boss. You don't mean that. These old boys work from can't see to can't see, and then some." He shook his head. "You just ain't got the reason to say that."

"Bull."

"That's what *I* say, boss, bull."

For a moment, Bill glared at Alkali, then shook his head and gave him a wry grin. "You're right. I just got in all a lather about last night."

A mischievous smile leaped to the skinny *segundo*'s lips. "I don't know why, boss. You looked kinda cute hopping all around like that."

Bill shot him a sheepish grin. "Yeah. Reckon I did make a fool out of myself."

"Naw. Not really. Ever'body just clammed up real fast and didn't give you much of a chance to make a fool of yourself." Alkali paused. "One good thing come of it though."

"What's that?" Bill arched an eyebrow.

Alkali nodded to the rancher's hat. "You got year-round cooling in your sombrero."

Bill rolled his eyes. "I swear you was kicked in the head when you were a yonker." He urged Bumpo into a trot. "Yep. I just played the fool. After all, it wasn't the girl's fault."

Alkali pulled in beside him. "Accidents happen. 'Course, from the look on her face, she figured you was going to come down on her stomping like a wild steer."

A twinge of embarrassment burned the rancher's ears. Dealing with women was sure creating a problem for him. They took all the certainty out of life. He had grown up reacting to events in a rough-and-tumble manner with little concern as to the other jasper's personal feelings. In the West, a man was a man, and if something bad happened to him, that was his own poor luck. He survived and made adjustments, or he simply died.

But now, toss a woman into the mix, and the soup took on a whole different look.

Alkali read his boss's mind. "Maybe you oughta let the girl know you ain't mad at her."

"Huh?" Bill glanced at Alkali blankly. Then his *segundo*'s words registered on him. "Oh, yeah, yeah. I reckon you might be right."

Shorty rode up and hooked his thumb over his shoulder. "Creek ahead, boss."

Bill pulled up. He'd forgotten about the creek. At least, he could get a bath. "Give 'em a break. Noon there."

Shorty wheeled around and headed back to the point. In the distance, the chuck wagon and Conestoga were approaching the tree-lined creek.

Bill brushed at his grimy shirt. He glanced at Alkali. "Keep 'em moving. I'm going to mend some fences."

Pancake had stopped in the shade of a spreading oak. Bill rummaged through his gear and fished out a clean shirt. He hesitated, then dug through his soogan once again. A shirt was missing. The red one. He shrugged. It was probably stuck back in a crack somewhere.

Swinging back into the saddle, Bill headed upstream for a bath.

After the nooning, Millie sat on the seat beside Ramón and stared out across the sweeping prairies ahead of them as the lumbering wagons moved ahead of the herd. The vastness of the prairie overwhelmed her. Compared to the confines of Boston, Texas was another universe, as different from the East as day from night.

The girls lay in their bunks, staring at the canvas ceiling above their heads. The rays of the sun suffused into a soft, yellow glow on the Osnaburg duck canvas.

Linitta glanced at her sister, knowing how hurt she had been the night before even though Uncle Bill had said nothing. But Millie had explained about him. He was raised by his older brother, her father. And she knew how her father could be.

A sharp knocking at the rear of the wagon startled Linitta. She sat up abruptly and saw her Uncle Bill looking at them through the pucker hole.

He grinned. "You girls want to go for a ride?"

For a moment, Linitta was speechless. Then she jumped to her feet and squealed. "Oh, yes, Uncle Bill. Oh, yes."

"Then get ready. I'll get your ponies." He paused and nodded to the front of the wagon. "And tell Millie I'll have Bumpo for her."

Chapter Thirteen

Ten minutes later, Shorty and Swede rode up leading the two pinto ponies, which they quickly saddled. Bill had switched to the black and handed Bumpo's reins to Millie. "Figured a ride would do us all some good," he said with a sheepish grin.

Millie studied him before stepping into the saddle from the Conestoga. He was wearing a fresh change of clothes, and he had scraped the three-day-old beard from his face. "You're probably right," she said. "A ride is just what we need."

He scooted around in the saddle and laid his hand on his saddlebags. "Pancake stuck some sourdough bullets and molasses in here. I figured we might find a spot where the girls would like a picnic."

Her eyebrows lifted in surprise. "A picnic? Why, Mr. Merritt. What's got into you?" Her eyes twinkled with merriment.

His cheeks colored. He shrugged. "Reckon I'm just trying to find some way to apologize to the little one, and to you and Linitta for the last few days. I haven't been the most hospitable jasper about."

Millie glanced at Linitta and Alwilda, who were settling into their saddles. She smiled at Bill. "I understand. Ramón has explained what this trip means. Even before we arrived," she added.

He pulled the black around. "A few miles ahead is a small spring in the middle of a grove of oaks."

"What about the herd?"

"Alkali's my foreman. He'll handle it."

Her eyes flashed. "What are we waiting for, then?"

The lush savannnas had given way to the short grass and sagebrush prairie that covered a rolling sea of hills, which stretched beyond the horizon to the Llano Estacado.

Bill had to admit all three were turning into fair riders. He had cautioned the girls to stay close, which they did, whooping and shouting as they rode in sweeping circles around Millie and him, raising clouds of white dust.

Behind, the herd trudged ever northward in its own billowing cloud of dust. Slowly the four drew away from the herd until the dust cloud seemed to lie on the undulating horizon.

Always a taciturn man, Bill responded to Millie's animated questions and remarks with terse monosyllables, but she accepted his brief replies in stride, for she had come to realize that in the West, a man's primary task was to maintain his concentration on the vast country through which they rode.

His eyes quartered the prairie around them, returning regularly to the girls. Not once did he look at Millie as they rode.

A squeal from Linitta jerked Bill's head around, and a grin popped on his face when he saw her take off after a scampering jackrabbit.

The darting rabbit cut in front of Nip and Alwilda. With a scream of delight, the younger sister joined in the pursuit.

Millie gasped, but Bill calmed her. ."Don't worry. They're okay. Just a little harmless fun."

"But . . . but what if they fall?"

Bill's grin broadened. "They'll hold on tighter next time."

She looked up at him in surprise. "That's kind of drastic, isn't it?"

"Maybe so," he replied. "But it's a mighty good teacher."

Straightening her slat bonnet, Millie shivered. The West was indeed an unforgiving land.

"Come on," he said, nudging the black into a trot. "Those two little dogies are almost out of sight." Both animals fell into a running two-step, gliding across the prairie.

The black gelding was a sound animal and smart too, but not like Bumpo; however, Bill reckoned that if he had to settle for an animal other than that jugheaded one, he could do a lot worse than the black.

Ahead, the girls pulled up and milled about, searching the thick buffalo grass for the jackrabbit that had suddenly vanished. A dark blur shot off at a right angle, and with a whoop and shout, the two girls took after it.

"They'll run its poor legs off," Millie said.

Bill chuckled. "Not a jackrabbit. Just watch. There's not many animals any sneakier than one of those Texas kangaroos."

No sooner had he replied than the girls pulled up, looking about for the rabbit.

Seconds later, the lanky jackrabbit, its long ears laid back, burst from beneath a sage, heading back in the direction from which it had come. For the next thirty minutes, the rabbit played hide-and-seek with the girls until Bill finally waved them in. It was midafternoon.

"Aw, we was having fun, Uncle Bill," Alwilda muttered, her face red from exertion.

He arched an eyebrow. "Remember what I told you when you got those ponies. You take care of them. Right now, they need a breather." He nodded to the horizon. "Yonder's the spring. I reckon we could all do with a drink of cold water."

In the cool shade cast by the live oaks, the girls tended their ponies, after which they removed their bonnets and washed their faces in the cool springwater before gobbling down the biscuits and molasses while Bill and Millie sat by the small fire and sipped fresh coffee.

She shivered with the first swallow of coffee. "Whew. I don't think I'll ever get used to your coffee. It's so strong, it puckers my lips."

The rawboned rancher laughed. "That's how we like it out here. Don't have time to squat and drink a potful. One cup's got to take care of a cowpoke for a few hours." He paused, then changed the subject. "With luck, we'll be hitting Abilene in a couple days. I figured on sending Ramón in to drop off those owlhoots' guns to Sam Cobb and pick up supplies."

Millie's face lit up. "Abilene? Is it a large town?"

"Well, for out here it is. Probably won't seem like much to you, seeing as how you're used to all those large cities and all back east."

He studied the girls, who were busy pouring molasses on another biscuit. "Figured on buying you ladies boots and hats. Doesn't seem quite sensible you out on horseback wearing bonnets and those little eastern shoes.''

Millie glanced at her high-top shoes. ''What's wrong with them?''

Bill shrugged. ''Yours, not much. You got a heel. The girls don't.''

''I don't understand.'' Millie frowned. ''What do heels have to do with anything?''

He pointed to the stirrup. ''Keeps your foot from slipping through. More'n one jasper's been drug to death when his foot got caught in the stirrup and the horse ran away with him.''

A chill ran up her arms, and she suddenly realized why he had been paying so much attention to the girls. ''It could happen to the girls?''

''Yep. Not likely though. That's why we tied the rawhide around the stirrup. Their feet can't slip through.''

Her eyebrows arched in understanding. ''I wondered about the rawhide. I couldn't see any sense in it, but I do now.''

Bill stiffened. He sniffed the air, then glanced at Bumpo, who was peering to the southwest, his ears pricked forward. Tuck whinnied. Rising quickly, Bill studied the clear sky to the west. The sun had dropped lower.

Alarmed, Millie came to stand beside him. ''What's wrong?''

''I'm not sure.''

The blistering sun had washed the blue out of the sky until it appeared almost white. Bill glanced at Bumpo. The stallion moved his feet nervously.

The wind switched to the southwest and immediately intensified. ''Blast,'' he muttered, sniffing the freshening breeze. He threw a quick glance in the direction of the herd, but the lead wagon was yet to roll across the southern horizon, another hour or so away.

"What's wrong?" Millie asked, her face growing pale.

He turned to her. "Quick. Mount up. You too, girls."

Millie grabbed his arm. "What is it? Tell us."

Bill pointed to the southwest. "Prairie fire. Faster than one of those locomotives you came out here on. Now, get in that saddle."

They swung into their saddles and milled about, awaiting instructions.

Bill hesitated, his eyes fixed on the distant horizon. A dark cloud rolled into view. He studied the cloud, a low-hanging line that appeared to be about twelve miles in length, stretching more to the south and southeast than the west. In the few seconds he watched, the cloud grew larger.

He reined the black around to face Millie and the girls. Alwilda's eyes brimmed with tears, but Linitta faced him with a set jaw. Bill forced a smile and spoke calmly. "Now, stay with me. These things move too fast for us to outrun, but it doesn't move sideways that fast. Our only chance is to go around it. Don't be scared. Just stay with me."

Millie forced a chuckle. "Don't worry, Bill. We'll be right with you, won't we, girls?"

Linitta nodded emphatically, but Alwilda remained motionless.

"One more thing, girls. Hold tight to the reins. Smoke spooks animals. If we hit a thick pocket of it, they might take the bit in their teeth. If that happens, yank hard. You understand?"

Alwilda choked out a reply. "Y-Yes, Uncle Bill."

"Look," Millie shouted, pointing to the southwest.

Bill grimaced. The flames were clearly visible now, leaping high into the air. "Let's go," he yelled, pointing the black due west, paralleling the fiery bank of smoke.

The entire prairie came alive with rabbits, coyotes, wolves, antelopes, even an occasional buffalo racing ahead of the oncoming fire. Tumbleweeds bounced through the sage.

His plan was to circle the western edge of the fire. If they failed, then he had to find them a refuge while the all-consuming flames roared past.

The smoke grew thicker. Bill's heart sank when they topped a rise and saw the fire moving west. He glanced over his shoulder. Tears from the smoke streamed down the girls' cheeks, but they kept their gallant little ponies right on the black's heels.

He kept them on their parallel course with the oncoming flames, but he had to hold in the black so the girls' ponies could keep pace. For every hundred yards the four riders covered, the firestorm leaped forward three hundred. Within a couple miles, the flames would be on them unless they turned tail, and then they couldn't hope to outrun the racing fire.

Although the roaring conflagration was fast approaching, the heat had not yet reached them, but, Bill knew, it was only a matter of minutes. He glanced at the ponies. Covered with lather, they were beginning to labor. The game little animals didn't have another ten minutes in them.

At the top of a rise, Bill reined up and peered out over the prairie. Beginning at the base of a sandhill to the north, a black line zigzagged to the south. "Come on," he yelled, driving the black forward.

In a stroke of luck, they had stumbled onto a dry arroyo. "This will take us through the fire," he exclaimed, bringing the black to a stiff-legged, sliding halt on the rim of the gully. A frown knit his brow and a curse rolled off his lips.

Tumbleweeds! Choking the windward side of the arroyo, which appeared to be about six feet deep, the brittle, dry bushes were more flammable than tinder. They burned with the intensity of black powder. A sudden explosion, a searing, intense fire, then ashes.

Without hesitation, he kicked the black down to the sandy bed of the arroyo. Filled with choking smoke, the sky grew darker. They milled about while Bill gave them instructions. "Follow me. When we reach the flames, you'll feel the heat, but there's no fire down here. We'll go slow at first, but when we get close to the flames, I'll give the signal. When I do, lay the leather to those ponies and keep your head down. You hear?"

The girls looked at each other in trepidation. Bill added, "Just do what I say. We'll be all right."

Millie forced a weak grin. "Okay."

"Let's go then."

The arroyo acted like a funnel for the smoke, drawing it along the sandy bed. Bill kept glancing at the tumbleweeds stacked along the side of the gully. If they should catch . . . He pushed the thought from his mind. They had enough to worry about now without borrowing trouble. Bill kept the black in a trot, conserving his energy for that final burst.

By now, they could feel the heat. Bill tugged his hat low over his eyes. With each twist and turn of the arroyo, the four drew ever closer to the raging fire. The roar of the fire beat against his ears like a thousand war drums. Great flames leaped into the air, startling yellows and red against a backdrop of black smoke. The acrid stench of burning sage stung his nose.

They rounded a bend and halted. Flames stretched high into the sky like the buttressed walls of a fort. The arroyo cut a narrow road through the raging inferno.

A chill raced through his blood. Ahead, tumbleweeds filled the gully, leaving only a narrow path. Sparks swirled and twisted, hurled high into the darkening sky by the turmoil of the firestorm before settling back down on the dried bushes. Within moments, the arroyo ahead would be an inferno.

They sky overhead was dark by now.

He pulled the black to a halt, but the leaping flames terrified the animal. The gelding jittered around, fighting against the reins. The nervous animal spooked the ponies. They milled about. Only Bumpo stood motionless despite the swirling sparks filling the air. The hot air whipped his mane.

Bill glanced fearfully at the tumbleweeds, then yelled above the roar of the fire. "All right, now listen. Stay right behind me, and don't stop driving those jugheads until we're away from the fire. Everybody hear?"

They nodded.

He hesitated and grinned at each of them. "Don't be afraid. Just stay with me, and whatever happens, keep whipping those animals." He reached over and tugged Alwilda's bonnet down. "We get to Abilene, I'll buy you a cowboy hat. How's that?"

The fear in her face faded. She smiled. "I'd like that."

"Okay." He wheeled the black around and dug his

heels into the gelding's flank. He yelled over his shoulder. "Let's go."

Bill hung tight in the saddle as the animal leaped forward, heading directly for the narrow pathway through the piles of tumbleweeds. He didn't look around, but he could hear the labored grunting of the ponies behind him. And then the roar of the inferno deafened him.

The heat grew intense. A sheet of sparks sprayed him. Just after he reached the tumbleweeds, the dried shrubs exploded into flames. In seconds, the arroyo became a living, savage beast leaping at the flying riders, hoping to drag them from their saddles.

One second, blistering flames threatened to boil his flesh, the next second, cool air rushed over him as he burst from the fire. He wheeled the black around in time to see two horses hurtle through a mass of writhing, curling flames.

"Millie! Millie!" Bill squinted into the flames and yelled. His only answer was the shriek of the fire.

Chapter Fourteen

Bill waited, expecting at every moment to see the hulking form of Bumpo burst from the fire, but all he saw were the raging flames.

The girls rode several yards beyond the rancher before yanking their ponies to a halt. Immediately they flailed at the sparks that had settled on their ponies and in their ponies and in their clothing. Then they realized Millie was missing.

Linitta pulled up beside Bill. "Where is she?"

He glanced at the girl, seeing the tears filling her frightened eyes. He looked back at the fire, which was a hundred yards away by now, and shook his head. All that was left were ashes winking in the growing darkness. "She's on Bumpo. He's too smart to get himself into something he can't get out of."

Bill paused, surprised to find that his words rang true in his own ears, because they were true. Sensing overwhelming odds, that roan stallion was smart enough to shy away at the last second. "Yeah," he added, forcing a grin. "Bumpo, he probably decided to find a better way out of this mess."

Satisfied by his explanation, Alwilda, who had ridden up, asked, "But, Uncle Bill, why didn't Nip or Tuck do like Bumpo?"

He chuckled. "These cayuses are nothing but knot-heads, dumb jugheads that would run off a cliff if you told them to. But Bumpo, he's got brains. Probably more'n me.''

Linitta snickered. "Oh, Uncle Bill. You don't mean that.''

He looked at her, then back at the fire. "Yep. If he did what I think he did, he's a far sight smarter than me.''

Stars winked through the thinning smoke. To the north, the fire continued, lighting the darkness with angry, dancing flames of red and yellow.

"Stay here. I'm going back,'' he said. Bumpo was smart, so he felt Millie was safe. Still, strange things happen, and if something had, he didn't want the girls to see it.

The sky was dark, but bits and pieces of sage still burned, tiny flames emitting a faint glow, enough to illumine the bed of the arroyo. Bill rode back along the gully, pausing by large piles of ashes, peering into shadowy niches, finally stopping where the four of them had drawn up just before their dash through the tumbleweeds.

Nothing.

Dismounting, Bill ground-reined the black and gathered a few charred branches to fashion a rough torch so he could study the sign.

"What are you looking for, Uncle Bill?''

The rancher glanced up to see the girls approaching. "I thought I told you girls to stay put.''

Alwilda looked over her shoulder at the dark arroyo behind her. "I was scared.''

He held the torch so the flickering flames lit their drawn and soot-stained faces. "Okay. Just stay where you are. I don't want the ground messed up.''

Linitta asked again, "What are you looking for, Uncle Bill?"

He kept his eyes fixed on the sandy bed. "Tracks. Trying to find out what happened, if I can. It's hard in sand." He held the torch closer to the sand where the bed had been torn. Sand had run back into the tracks, but from the depth of the tracks and the ones leading to the right, it was obvious a horse had recently shied away from the fire and headed back up the arroyo.

The tracks had to be Bumpo's. "Here they are," he told the girls, holding the torch at the scars in the sand.

"How can you tell they're Millie's, Uncle Bill?"

He kept his eyes on the tracks while he explained. "We rode right over the spot not ten minutes ago. If this track had been here, we would have torn it up. No, this track was made in the last few minutes. Bumpo is the only one who could have made it."

He held the torch to the ground and followed the sign. It led back up the arroyo, to the north. He shook his head. He could do no more tonight.

"Okay, girls. Looks like we'll spend the night here. That cut over there looks like it'll work." He nodded to a narrow draw that carried runoff into the arroyo.

Linitta frowned. "Why can't we go on tonight, Uncle Bill?"

"I want to, girls. Believe me, but it's too dark. If Millie is lying hurt in the shadows, we could go right past her. Miss her completely. As much as I hate to say it, our best bet to help her is wait until we can see what we're doing. You understand?"

The girls looked at each other. They nodded to each other. "We understand, Uncle Bill," Linitta said.

After hobbling the horses, Bill spread a tarp and put

together a small fire. He tossed his saddlebags and canteen on the tarp. "At least we won't starve. Biscuits and
molasses."

Bill slept in snatches, worried about Millie and worried about the herd. He knew the fire stampeded it, but
he knew also that Alkali was the best *segundo* a rancher
could have. He'd save as many head as he could, and if
they had to, they could stay put for a few days to round
up all the strays.

Just before Bumpo reached the passage through the
tumbleweeds, the dried brush had exploded into flames.
Without hesitation, he leaped to the right.

Millie felt herself slipping from the saddle. She
clutched the saddle horn with both hands. Her head
popped back, and she felt her fingers losing their grip as
Bumpo raced back up the arroyo. The wind blew sand
into her eyes, blinding her.

Clenching her teeth, she yanked herself forward and
sprawled across the pommel, intertwining her fingers in
Bumpo's mane and stiffening in the stirrups as he
lurched from the arroyo and burst into an all-out sprint
for the darkness to the north.

Her legs began to ache. Stabbing pains shot through
her side, but she clenched her teeth against the pain. She
could still feel the heat of the fire on her back. Bill had
been right. The inferno consumed the prairie faster than
a locomotive. She just prayed Bumpo wouldn't stumble.
Millie gripped his mane tighter, praying she could remain in the saddle.

The great stallion sped across the prairie almost effortlessly, eating up the miles until the leaping flames
dropped below the horizon. Millie shot a glance over her

shoulder. The fire lit the dark sky with a pale glow. Bumpo continued his pace.

He flashed over a hill, past a small patch of head-high shinnery, then angled to the northwest. His nostrils flared. He picked up the scent of water.

Millie had lost all sense of direction. Though her eyes stung from the smoke and sand, she felt the change of direction. She managed to squint into the darkness ahead, but she saw nothing, just the blurred silhouettes of sage dotting the dimly lit prairie at their feet.

Her slat bonnet had blown off and flapped against her back. Her fingers cramped, but she refused to release her grip on Bumpo's mane. Minutes ran together. She lost track of time.

Suddenly, Bumpo slowed to a lope, then to a trot. Millie peered into the night. A dark mass rose from the prairie ahead of her. The stallion headed straight for it.

Minutes later, they entered a small grove of oaks, and Bumpo stopped. Millie glimpsed the starlight reflecting off a small creek. ''So this is what you had in mind, huh?'' she said, patting the lathered neck of the stallion. ''You think this will stop the fire?''

Bumpo lowered his head and drank. Millie arched an eyebrow. ''I guess you do.'' She dismounted and knelt beside Bumpo. She drank deeply, after which she loosened her neckerchief and washed her face.

To the south, the fire was rolling over the horizon.

She waded the creek with Bumpo, who began grazing on the lush grass. ''Well, if you're not worried, I'm not either.''

Millie straightened her bonnet and sat against a large oak. She knew Bill would take care of the girls. Come morning, she and Bumpo would find their way back to the herd. She closed her eyes for a moment. In the next instant, she was sound asleep.

Bumpo's whinny prodded her awake. She raised her head, groaning as she rubbed the crick in the back of her neck. She had slept with her chin resting on her chest.

Bumpo whinnied again. "All right, all right," she muttered, blinking the sleep from her eyes. "I'll get . . ." She looked up and froze.

Leering down at her were six Indians, one of whom wore Bill's red shirt.

Far to the south, Linitta's eyes popped open and in the dim glow of the campfire, she watched a June bug scurry over the sand inches from her face. She lay motionless on her side, her knees drawn up, her hands folded prayerlike under her cheek, watching the bug scamper around. Then a mouth-watering aroma tickled her nose.

She sat up. Uncle Bill was cooking some breakfast. Chunks of meat roasted on spits over the small fire. Her stomach rumbled. She nudged Alwilda and climbed to her feet.

She brushed the sand from her clothes. "Smells good, Uncle Bill."

He looked around and grinned. "Rabbit. Nice and crisp." He pulled off a chunk and popped it in his mouth. "Dig in. We need to get after Millie and Bumpo as soon as we can."

Eagerly the girls squatted by the fire. Bill pointed to the spits stuck in the sand. "Just pick one up and eat the chunks off the end. "That's all there is to it."

"I never ate rabbit before, Uncle Bill. Is it good?" Alwilda asked.

Bill nodded to the spit. "Try it and see. There's a couple dry biscuits left if you don't like it."

Linitta studied the roasted white chunks of meat. They smelled wonderful. Tentatively she bit into one. It was sweet and tender, sort of like chicken, she thought. "It is good," she said, popping the rest of the chunk in her mouth.

Bill had prepared half a dozen spits with four chunks on each. In ten minutes, they were picked clean.

"Rabbit sure is good," Alwilda said, taking a drink from the canteen.

"It sure is," Linitta echoed.

Bill rose. "Okay, girls. Mount up. We've got to find Millie."

As they headed north up the arroyo, Alwilda licked her lips. "Did you like the rabbit, Linitta."

The older girl's eyes twinkled and she patted her stomach. "Sure did. Do you think Mr. Pancake would cook us some, Uncle Bill? I mean, if we asked him real nice."

"I reckon he will, girls. I reckon he will." The raw-boned rancher grinned and glanced at the rattlesnake skin he had thrown away earlier.

Having risen at false dawn, Bill had tracked Bumpo a half-mile to where the roan stallion exited the arroyo. He led the girls up the arroyo at a trot to the narrow gully cutting up to the prairie.

As far as the eye could see, the prairie was black. The acrid stench of burned sage hung in the air. Bill followed the sign a few yards and then it was lost in the soot and ashes.

"What's wrong, Uncle Bill?"

He looked at Linitta and shook his head. "The fire

wiped out everything. All we know is they headed north, away from the fire.''

Alwilda sobbed. ''C-Can't we go find her?''

''Not yet. We got the herd to think about. Besides, we got no grub, almost out of water. Best thing is for us to get back to the herd and then I'll resupply and find her.''

The small girl's bottom lip quivered. ''No. I want Millie.''

Linitta tried to calm her. ''Uncle Bill's right. Millie could be anywhere. We don't know where to start looking.''

Alwilda stared defiantly at her sister. ''No.''

Bill's deep voice growled. ''You'll do what I say, girl, or I'll tan your rear.''

The defiance fled her face.

He nodded. ''Now, follow me.'' Without another word, he headed east. He didn't know which he wished for the most, the end of the drive or getting rid of the girls.

Obediently Alwilda followed. Linitta brought up the rear, a big grin on her face.

The farther Bill rode, the more apprehensive he became. The prairie fire had ranged far and wide. They paused at the spring where they had picnicked the day before. The fire had burned around it.

At noon, Bill spotted a low-hanging cloud of dust to the northeast. Upon topping a rise, he spotted the wagons near a grove of burned trees. He groaned. The herd was spread as far as the eye could see.

They rode on in. Alkali came out to meet them. ''We figured you was okay, boss, but. . . .'' He paused, his eyes searching behind Bill and the girls. "Where's Miss Millie? Where's Bumpo?"

Bill motioned the girls on to the wagons while he and Alkali remained behind. He related their story. "Now what about here?"

"Not real good, boss. We got about twenty-five hundred rounded up. If we had some graze, we could hang around a couple days, but all we got is a creek ahead. I sent Shorty out to see if there's graze beyond. There should be unless the fire leaped the water."

The rancher removed his hat and wiped the sweat and grit from his face. "You did right. Leave a couple old boys behind to round up strays. Push on to some graze. Rest up there until you've picked up as much stock as you can."

"Okay. What about you?"

"I'm going out for Miss Millie. She's on Bumpo, so I'm not worried about the fire as much as who she might run into out there. Who can you spare to go with me?"

Alkali twisted up one side of his lips in a grimace. "They're all good boys, boss. Why don't you take Catman? I reckon if I had to pick one to ride the river with, he'd be it."

Bill nodded. "Tell him to get ready. I'm riding out in ten minutes. Just you keep them going. Something happens to me, sell the beef in Dodge, pay off the ranch, and look after them girls till some old maid aunt gets back in the country in a couple months."

"Don't worry, boss. We'll be waiting for you."

Before the rancher rode out, he swung by the Conestoga and told the girls where he was going.

"D-Do you think Millie is all right?" Linitta's tiny voice was frail and tentative.

He forced a broad grin. ''Sure. She's riding Bumpo. Nothing ever happens to that jughead.''

The girls laughed.

Bill nodded to Ramón and Pancake. ''The boys here will take care of you. Just don't you cause them no trouble. You hear?''

The girls nodded. ''Yes, Uncle Bill.''

Alwilda piped up. ''Uncle Bill, can we go riding while you're looking for Millie?''

He shot a sidelong glance at Ramón, who arched an eyebrow in amusement. ''Not right away. Alkali's got to get the herd to some graze. They won't have time to look after you girls.''

Linitta stepped forward and took her sister's hand. ''Don't worry, Uncle Bill. We'll behave ourselves.''

Bill studied them a few seconds, then nodded. ''You better.''

Chapter Fifteen

Ten minutes later, the two cowboys rode out, a tall, lanky rancher burned almost black by the sun, and a thick-bearded cowpoke with eyes sunk deep in his scrawny head. His normally gray beard was stained black by soot and tobacco.

"What do you figure on doing, Bill?" They rode side by side in a mile-eating lope.

"Start where I lost the sign. I figure she headed north, but we need to be sure."

Catman nodded and settled back in his saddle, falling into the rhythmic movement of his pony, a habit that had come from fifty years forking horses.

Behind them, black dust rose into the pale sky as Alkali pushed the herd north, seeking water and grass. Ahead, the prairie lay black and desolate. The southwest wind picked up, and to the northwest, a dust devil danced across the short grass and sage prairie.

"Here it is," Bill said, nodding toward the faint sign on the rim of the arroyo. The wind had all but erased the tracks.

Catman clucked his tongue. "Ain't much to go on."

Bill didn't reply. His sharp eyes picked up the trail. "Heads west."

The older man rode ahead. "Cuts back north here. Like you figured. She decided to outrun the fire."

147

For a moment, Bill didn't answer.

Catman arched an eyebrow. ''Don't you figure so?''

''No. I figure it was Bumpo, not her. She's a tenderfoot. I figure had it been up to her, she'd have followed me and the girls through the tumbleweeds. It was Bumpo. For some reason, he backed out.''

''Ain't no animal that smart. I know you set quite store by that broomtail, but he's just a hardheaded saddle bronc like the rest. If he backed away from the fire, it was because he got scared.''

Bill shook his head. The degree of Bumpo's intelligence was the subject of an ongoing argument between the two, had been for five years. ''One of these days, Catman, you'll eat those words.''

They made slow progress, for the sign became more and more difficult to cut. Finally, they lost it altogether. Bill grimaced. ''We're not going to find anything. We've been looking for an hour.''

Catman shrugged. ''She was headin' north.''

Bill nodded. ''Yep.''

With the wind at their backs, the two headed north, across the vast, undulating prairie that lay before them like a great black carpet, a carpet that would be turning green within the next couple days. Wildfires were nature's way of reconditioning the soil. Bill had been witness to the miracle more than once. After a fire, the grass came back greener, thicker, taller.

The sun crept closer to the horizon, painting the western sky with deep purples and gaudy pinks. ''Reckon we need to find a spot to bed down,'' Bill muttered.

''Yep,'' Catman drawled, squirting a stream of tobacco on the ground as his light blue eyes scanned the rolling hills for some kind of protection against the southwest wind. "But I don't see no place to hunker down. At least, no place out of this wind."

"There's a spot." Bill pointed to a patch of head-high shinnery on the side of a hill. "The fire left some of it standing. At least we'll have some firewood."

Millie lay on her side, feigning sleep, listening carefully as the Kiowas, their numbers increased by newcomers, carried on a heated discussion around the campfire. She had been pushed around once or twice, but she hadn't been mistreated.

They'd even offered her some grub, which she declined after she smelled it even through her stomach growled. She knew she was the center of the discussion, for several times throughout the day, a gesticulating brave would point at her and return to the discussion.

Although she was a bright young woman, Millie had no idea what was taking place until she spotted the remuda of Indian ponies. A few pieces of the puzzle fell together. They were Kiowa, a fact she had determined simply by asking. Then there was the red shirt. And now the ponies.

At first, she refused to permit herself to even ask the question, but the longer she considered the few pieces of evidence, however uncertain, the more the clues seemed to fit together. Kiowa, red shirt, ponies. Her eyes narrowed. That had to be the answer.

She peered into the darkness in the direction of the remuda. How many ponies were out there? Twenty-four? No. If she was right, there would be at least thirty-two. One pony for each Kiowa brave, and twenty-four to pay Bill Merritt's price, the price he had jokingly placed on her head back in South Texas!

She muttered under her breath. "When I get my hands

on him, I'll . . . I'll . . .'' She couldn't think of anything horrible enough. "But I will," she whispered. "I promise."

Millie tried to remain awake, but the rigors of the last few days had been too strenuous. She dozed. During the night, the sound of hoofbeats awakened her. The remuda was moving out, but why? If she were right, the ponies were to be used as payment for her. So why take them without her? Maybe the Kiowa had decided to keep the ponies since they already had her.

She heard a snuffle from the darkness in front of her. Bumpo. He was watching her.

Millie couldn't resist smiling at how Bumpo had buffaloed the Kiowa. They tried to put him in their remuda, but he had immediately stampeded the ponies and returned to her side. Later, a brave leaped onto his back, and Bumpo promptly ran him under a limb, busting his nose, scraping the unfortunate brave up pretty bad before returning to Millie's side. That had been enough for the Kiowa, great horsemen that they were.

Any animal so devoted to its owner was revered by the Kiowa.

The white woman could keep him.

Bill and Catman moved out at false dawn, heading north. The sky was clear, promising a scorcher. The wind had quartered to the south during the night. The older cowboy squirted a stream of tobacco juice and drawled. "We git past the fire, maybe we can find something."

"Maybe. We'll see. No telling how far it burned."

"I've seen 'em stop for no practical reason, just like I've seen 'em start."

Three hours later, Bill squinted to the northwest. "Looks like trees. Maybe a spring."

Catman followed his gaze. "Your eyes are better'n mine," he replied. "I can't tell what it is. Besides, I . . . Hold it. What's that up ahead?"

Bill spotted the sign just as Catman spoke, a broad trail across the burned prairie headed to the southeast.

The two men quickly read the sign.

"Twenty-five, maybe thirty ponies. Four or five mounted. What do you think, Bill?" Catman looked at his boss.

"Indian. No question, but what are they up to?" He looked up the back trail. It appeared to lead directly to the stand of trees on the horizon. He considered backtracking to the trees, but there was no sign of life—no smoke, dust, or anything to indicate someone was there.

Catman turned southeast. "Let's follow these Injuns. That's the only way to find out what they're up to. Maybe they seen her."

Deep within the stand of oaks, tears of anger filled Millie's eyes as she struggled against the grasp of the Kiowa brave who had grabbed her around the waist and clapped his hand over her mouth when he spotted the riders.

She flailed her arms and legs, watching helplessly as the two riders hesitated, then headed after the remuda. In frustration, she bit the Kiowa's fingers.

He shouted and released her, but before she could shout, a crushing blow knocked her senseless. She struggled to retain consciousness, but she slipped deeper and deeper into a dark hole.

Unnoticed by the Kiowa braves, Bumpo's ears perked forward at the distant movement across the prairie. The southerly breeze twisted and curled through the tree, bringing the roan stallion a familiar smell.

He whinnied.

One of the Kiowa hurried to him, grabbing the lead rope tied to a limb. Before the brave could take a step, Bumpo laid his ears back and charged, ripping the rope from the limb. The Kiowa jumped back, banged into a tree trunk, and bounced forward to the ground, unconscious.

The remaining Kiowa ran forward, a leather lariat in hand. He shook out a loop and whirled it around his head. He released the rope. A perfect loop arched through the air toward Bumpo, who charged the loop and ran over the Kiowa.

Bumpo slid to a halt and shook his head, slinging the loop from his neck. He nuzzled Millie, but she was unconscious. He looked across the prairie at the riders. With a whinny, he raced after them.

"What the blazes is that?" Catman said, glancing over his shoulder.

Bill scooted around in the saddle. As soon as he saw the gait of the fast-approaching horse, he shouted. "Bumpo! It's Bumpo!"

The roan stallion nuzzled up to Bill, who fumbled to untie the lead rope that was dragging the ground. Trying to still the cold fear in his chest, he nodded to the trees. "That's where he came from, Catman. And I'll bet you dollars to donuts that's where Millie is." He dug his spurs into the black and laid leather across the animal's rump.

Millie was still unconscious when they arrived, but a drink of fresh water revived her. She glanced around, confused. "The Indians . . . There were two of them."

Bill and Catman searched the small grove of oaks. No Kiowas. But they found fresh sign indicating two ponies had recently ridden out to the northwest. There was blood on the ground by the sign.

"All I remember is seeing you and Catman riding away. Next thing I knew, you were waking me."

Bill grunted and glanced up at Bumpo. "If you could only talk."

Bumpo whinnied.

They reached the herd just before dusk. All the cowpokes except the nighthawks gathered around the fire after supper, anxious to hear Millie's tale, but the combination of exhaustion, a full stomach, and a warm fire was too much for her. Within minutes after she ate, she fell asleep.

Her story had to wait until the next night, and after she told it, and voiced her suspicions about the purpose of the remuda, Bill closed his eyes and groaned.

Several punchers snickered at his discomfort.

"I reckon you're probably right," he admitted. "At the time, it was the easy way out of that situation. I never figured they'd take me serious." He paused and grinned mischievously. "I reckon they set store by your red hair."

It was Millie's turn to squirm. Her cheeks colored. "Twenty-four horses. Is that all I'm worth?"

Alkali chimed in. "Why, that's quite a heap, Miss Millie. Injuns put a lot of value on their horses. A rich man has only twelve or thirteen. To be honest, it's unheard of for any Injun to offer twenty-four ponies for anything, even a Winchester '76."

She gave them a wry grin. "Well, it's nice to know that at least I'm worth a Winchester '76."

The entire camp laughed.

Bill couldn't remember when he felt so content.

"But it was Bumpo who deserves the credit. There were two Kiowa there when I spotted Bill and Catman. I don't know what happened to them," she added.

Bill glanced at Catman and grinned. "What'd I tell you about that horse?"

The older cowpoke grunted. "I still say he's just a jugheaded saddle bronc that's got nothing but mud between the ears."

Pushing to his feet, Bill chuckled. "Well, old friend. At least he's got something between the ears."

The camp laughed again.

The herd pushed out next morning. They'd lost only twenty head, although the fire had probably run about twenty or thirty thousand pounds of fat off the beeves. "We'll just take it easy and they'll gain most of it back by the time we hit Dodge," Bill said.

Two days later, Bill sent Ramón into Abilene. Although he wanted to go in himself, he knew the other hands deserved a treat. In his place, he sent Snag and Pump with orders to drop off the hardware to Sam Cobb and look after Millie and the girls. "I promised them boots and hats. And by the way," he whispered to Ramón, "bring back half a dozen bottles for the boys."

"*Sí*, Mr. Bill. Do not worry."

"Catch up with us, but be careful."

"*Sí*, Mr. Bill. Ramón, he will be careful."

The next evening, the crew returned from Abilene with the supplies, the girls with new hats and boots, which they eagerly modeled for the punchers around the campfire.

"You get the whiskey?" Bill asked Ramón.

"*Sí*. In the wagon."

Bill rose and dusted off his jeans. "Okay, boys. We got us a delicate situation here. I reckon I can speak to you about it, and you'll handle it like the men you are.

We got ladies present, and I know you've all done your mightiest to use good language and such. Usually, us men leave the women and go into another room or out on the porch for our after-dinner drink, but seeing as we got no other room or porch to retire to, I expect you to continue being the gentlemen you have been. I got a treat for you boys tonight. Grab your cups. Pancake's dishing out Old Crow—good Kentucky whiskey. One cup per man. Any jasper acts up, and he's got me to answer to. Like I said, we have ladies present, and I expect us to remember that fact.''

Millie rose. ''The girls and I can retire to the wagon, Bill.''

He shook his head. ''No, ma'am. Not unless you prefer to. Sometimes by ourselves, we get rowdy. But that's just boys showing off. We got men working here. Right, boys?''

A round of laughter greeted his remarks.

Millie and the girls remained by the fire, chatting and laughing with the punchers who, to a man, sipped their whiskey with exaggerated decorum.

Alkali took Bill aside. ''Boss, Snag talked to Sergeant Sam Cobb of the Texas Rangers in Abilene.''

''They tried those rustlers yet?''

''That's what Sam sent word about. Their leader, Waco Brown, the one who threatened you . . . well, him and six of his men broke out of jail last night. Sam says for you to keep your eyes open. Gettin' back at you was all that jasper talked about.''

Bill took a long drink of whiskey. He shook his head and stared at the stars. What next?

Chapter Sixteen

Bill put out extra guards, but the night passed without incident. "Maybe Waco was just talking, boss," Alkali said over morning coffee.

"Maybe. But, don't count on it. I never knew a man who got snakebit when he was expecting it. We'll keep extra men out at night."

Two days later, the herd crossed the main fork of the Brazos and pushed on toward Doan's Crossing on the Red River. One day rolled into the next—hot, dusty, and tedious. And each evening, Bill Merritt breathed a sigh of relief. Another fifteen or twenty miles and no trouble. Waco Brown slowly receded into the past.

Occasional storms rumbled across the prairie, soaking the ground and cooling the air. The punchers kept a wary eye on the storms. Most were gentle rain showers. Once or twice on the distant horizon, lightning crackled and danced, but luck was with the Bar Slashes, for the fickle hands of nature seemed to be guiding the electrical storms away from the herd.

Still, Bill was worried about the unusual number of storms. One or two a month during the summer was average for the watershed of the Red River. Two a week disturbed the rancher. "The Red's bad enough at low water," he muttered to Alkali as they observed a shower

156

on the horizon move across their trail. "Many an hombre buried along its banks'll testify to that."

"Reckon I know what you mean, boss. My first time through here was with the Sisker outfit from up above old Fort Brown. Bob Sisker, the old man's youngest, got tangled under some spooked steers and drowned." Alkali shook his head. "The old man just seemed to die himself. Never was the same afterward."

Bill watched the distant storm. "Right now, I'd settle for a blazing sun and a scorching wind."

"Me too," Alkali said. "Me too."

But the unusual weather continued.

When they hit the Red at Doan's Crossing, it was full from bank to bank, three hundred yards wide. The waterline on the red bluffs and the debris in the willows indicated that the river was falling.

"Lordy," Shorty Wilson muttered. "It must've been eight or nine feet deep."

Snag Podecker nodded. "Looks like it."

"We got no choice," Bill said, observing the muddy river from his saddle. "We've got to wait till it drops. Couple days if we don't have any more rain." He glanced back to the south, his forehead knit with uneasiness.

Alkali caught the glance. "Waco?"

Bill gave him a wry grin. "Yeah. I got the feeling that jasper is out there somewhere."

"We can handle him, boss." Alkali patted the butt of his six-gun. "Don't worry about that."

For the next two days, the herd milled about, stripping the countryside of every twig of grass as the river slowly dropped.

Around the fire the second evening, Millie and the girls sat on a driftlog and watched the river. Sandbars had begun to appear in the rush of muddy water. "What happened to all the water, Uncle Bill?" Linitta frowned as she asked the question.

He sipped his coffee. "Dry country. Normally, there's only two or three channels out there. You'll see them in the morning. When there's heavy rain upcountry, the river'll flood, but it goes down just as fast as it rises."

Her face taut with concern, Millie studied the river. "Those channels, are they deep?"

"Not usually. Sometimes we'll hit a swimming channel, but for the most part, they're no more than ten, twelve inches. What we've got to be most concerned about is quicksand, but here at Doan's Crossing, it isn't likely."

Linitta looked up at him. "Quicksand? What's that?"

Bill looked at Millie, who was staring hard at him, her face pale. "It's a patch of sand with water under it. It won't pack down. You step in it, and you'll sink."

Alwilda spoke up. "All the way?"

He shook his head. "Not if you're smart. You'll sink so far, then stop. You struggle, you can sink deeper. That's why, if you ever hit any quicksand, fall back the way you came. You'll stay on top, and if you swim real slow with your arms, you can pull yourself from the sand."

By now, Millie was visibly alarmed. Bill directed his next words to her. "You've seen by now that we face some kind of danger every day out here. Rattlesnakes, Indians, outlaws, the weather . . . These girls, they'll be better off knowing what to expect. You will too."

Millie chewed on her lip and looked out across the river. "How . . . how will you get the wagons across?"

Alkali, who had been listening, grunted and turned back to the coffeepot. Bill arched an eyebrow and gave her a wry grin. "Usually, the wheels sink. We'll loop on as many lassos as we need to haul it across. It's built of wood, so it can't sink, but it can sure as blazes get stuck mighty tight."

She glanced at Alkali, who nodded.

"So, what you're telling us is that tomorrow could be exciting?"

Bill pursed his lips and considered her question. "Or boring. Seems like that's how it is out here, either boring as knitting socks or exciting as a tornado."

Millie forced a laugh. She glanced around at the stark countryside. "You keep calling this Doan's Crossing."

The rawboned rancher nodded. "Used to be a trading post here. Back west a short piece. Ed Doan run it. Story I got was that Comanche killed him. Might be true, might not. But that's where the name come from."

She ran her fingers through her red hair and stared at the stars overhead. Didn't anything pleasant ever happen out here?

The next morning dawned bright and clear. The river had dropped even more, and as Bill had predicted, three narrow channels twisted down the river, one in the middle, and the other two on the far side. The herd was ready to move.

Millie looked across the river, noting the tracks leading toward the first channel. "The boss," Alkali drawled, "he was out before the sun, finding a safe trail across."

She looked again and spotted two rows of branches stuck in the sand, marking the breadth of the trail curving across the expansive bed of sand.

Water dripping from his boots and Bumpo's belly, Bill reined up at the shoreline and waved the chuck wagon forward. "No swimming today, boys. Sand's firm, but don't lollygag around."

With a shout, four punchers looped their lariats on the wagon and fanned out ahead, careful to remain within the sticks on either side of the trail.

The chuck wagon hit the sandy bed at a trot. Ramón drew the Conestoga up to the shoreline and waited. Millie held her breath as Pancake shouted at his team. She gasped when once, a rear wheel began sinking. In the next instant, the straining horses yanked it free before the sand could grab it.

Minutes later, the chuck wagon rolled up the far bank amid the cheers of the elated cowboys. Coiling their lariats, the riders dashed back across the river for the Conestoga.

Millie and the girls held on tight as the heavy wagon hit the bed on the run and moved effortlessly across the sand and through the channels until it reached the far shore.

Bill rode up with a big grin. "See. Simple as stomping ants." He wheeled Bumpo around and shouted at Alkali. "Get the herd moving. We're wasting time."

The Bar Slashes lumbered into Indian Territory, an unending panorama of rolling hills and treeless plains. For two days, the herd, like a great brown serpent, snaked over and around the sand hills dotting the short grass prairie.

"Are we in danger of Indian attacks?" Millie asked

the question around the campfire their first night into the territory. Linitta and Alwilda were at her shoulder, their wide eyes locked on Bill Merritt.

He shrugged. "No more'n usual. Truth is, probably not as much danger. This part of the country was set aside by the U.S. government for the friendly tribes like the Cohoctaws, Chickasaws, the Cherokees, and others. Past few years, some Comanche and Kiowa have come in. They're usually the troublemakers. But, when their young bucks decide to leave the reservation, they usually head deep into the state, down around Austin or San Antone. They don't hanker to stir up trouble around their own front door."

Linitta glanced into the darkness and shivered. "They scare me, Uncle Bill."

He stared at her for several seconds, suddenly realizing just how vunerable she really was, just how much she depended on him. He spoke in a soft, gentle voice. "Nothing wrong with being scared, girl. Keeps a man— or a woman—on his toes. Out here, it's the careless man, or the foolish man, who gets himself hurt. The jasper who keeps his eyes open will manage to keep his hair."

His answer seemed to satisfy the girls, for they sat on the ground beside Millie and stared into the flames licking up around the coffeepot.

Bill sat back on his heels and cupped his coffee mug in two hands. He shot a glance at Millie, who returned it with a smile. A warm feeling of satisfaction flooded over him.

Midmorning, three days out from the Red River, a cloud of dust arose on the eastern horizon. Not an eye among the Bar Slash riders missed it. Throughout the day, the cloud grew closer, and the punchers grew restless. Six-guns were checked and double-checked. Saddle rifles were loaded.

At noon, Bill refused the girls' request to ride, insisting they remain in the Conestoga as it moved ahead to the evening camp.

"What do you think, boss?" Alkali stood in his stirrups and studied the cloud, which in midafternoon began moving parallel with the herd at a distance of about four or five miles.

"I figure we ought to find out what's stirring up that dust and why it turned north on us."

"Injuns, you think?"

"Doubt it. They wouldn't be waving a flag like that," he said, referring to the cloud of dust rising into the clear sky. Wheeling about, he ordered Shorty to keep the herd moving.

With Alkali at his side, the lanky rancher cut across the prairie to intersect the cloud of dust, taking care to remain out of sight by riding around the sand hills instead of over the crest.

Suddenly, Bill reined up.

At the base of a sand hill, a Kiowa brave sat motionless in his saddle, facing the two cowboys. He held his hand over his head in a sign of peace.

Bill blinked his eyes. The warrior was wearing Bill's missing shirt, the red one.

Back in camp that evening, the rawboned rancher squatted by the fire and sipped his coffee while everyone waited expectantly for him to speak. Alkali stood behind him, an amused grin on his sunburned face.

"It was the Kiowa," he announced. "That same bunch we crossed down Texas."

Millie gasped.

Ramón, who was greasing the rear wheel on the chuck wagon, paused and looked around. He set the bucket of tallow on the ground beside the Conestoga.

Bill continued. "That's right. The same bunch, and they have twenty-four horses with them."

A couple cowpokes snickered, and Bill nailed them with a steely look. He cleared his throat and continued. "I told them I'd changed my mind."

Millie leaned forward. "What did they say then?"

Bill shifted uncomfortably and glanced at Alkali, who quickly began studying the ground at his feet. "They said it wasn't up to me. They were coming into camp in the morning."

She glanced around at the suddenly somber faces. "What does that mean? Who is it up to?"

Taking a deep breath, Bill looked her in the eyes. "You. You see, in their courting period, the—"

Millie shook her head. "Courting! Who's courting? I'm not courting!"

Pancake broke in. "Makes no difference to the Kiowa, Miss Millie. The man courts. The woman just waits."

Her eyes narrowed. "Why, that's . . . that's idiotic."

"Maybe so," Bill said. "But, you see, the Kiowa believes if the woman agrees, then her owner . . ." He hesitated and winced at the murderous gleam in her eyes. "I don't mean it that way," he hastily explained. "But that's how the Kiowa looks at it. If the woman is agreeable, the owner or father has no say so. He must take the agreed-upon price."

Alwilda looked up at Millie. "What does Uncle Bill mean, Millie?"

The young woman glared at the rancher. Her voice

shook with anger. "He means he stuck his foot in his mouth back in Texas and still hasn't figured how to get it out." She jumped to her feet and shook her finger at Bill Merritt. "I'll tell you one thing, Mr. Merritt. You'd better figure some way out of this by the time those wild heathens get here, or I'll cause you so much trouble, you'll think that stampede was nothing more than a temper tantrum thrown by a two-year-old brat."

She glared at the cowpokes, every one of whom ducked his head. She grabbed the girls' hands. "Come, children. Let's go to bed and let the men, in all their collective wisdom, solve the problems they created."

After she disappeared into the Conestoga, Alkali whistled. "I don't reckon I ever seen a woman so mad. Just, ah, what are you going to do, boss?"

Bill frowned up at his *segundo.* "Me? Why should I do anything?"

Pancake chuckled. " 'Cause you're the jasper she's going to shoot."

During the midnight-shift nighthawking, Bill rode out to check the herd. He fell in beside his *segundo.*

"Couldn't sleep, huh, boss?" Alkali greeted him jovially.

"Nope. Too much on my mind."

"The girl?"

"I reckon."

"You figure the Kiowa are going to raise Cain?"

"Not right away. They don't want no shooting, so I figure they'll tag along and steal a few head when they get the chance. Make a nuisance of themselves."

"Probably right. Those bucks won't take too kindly

to being turned down. Kiowa are proud people. Most squaws would be right pleased to join the tribe.''

Bill chuckled. ''Not this one. We'll hold the herd here until they come in and settle their business. That way, we got us a few six-guns handy.''

''I got you, boss. Don't worry.''

Chapter Seventeen

To Bill's surprise, the lantern in the Conestoga was lit when he reached the campfire next morning. He knocked on the side of the wagon.

Millie's voice was sharp and cold. "Yes?"

Bill cleared his throat. "It's best if you and the girls stay in the wagon when the Kiowa come in."

She snapped back at him. "Don't worry about us, Mr. Merritt. Just you handle the mess you made."

The rawboned rancher cringed at her words and returned to the fire where he poured a cup of coffee and squatted on his heels, staring at the wagon. Millie and the girls were moving around, and the lantern was casting distorted shadows on the canvas. From time to time, he heard a giggle. He frowned. What the blazes was going on in there? Slowly, more punchers joined him at the fire, expectantly awaiting the arrival of the Kiowa.

Soon the shadows on the canvas stopped moving, and as the sun rose, the lantern was extinguished.

Snag looked at Catman and nodded to the wagon as if to ask what was going on. The older man stroked his beard and squirted a stream of tobacco juice on the ground. "Beats me." The entire camp grew silent, the only sound the crackling of the fire.

The rumble of hooves broke the silence. As one, the punchers rose and faced the oncoming remuda, which

166

pulled up a short piece from the camp. Four Kiowa braves rode forward, erect and proud, hair pulled back and fastened with eagle talons, dressed in all their finery, breastplates of bone, necklaces of bear teeth.

They halted several yards from the camp. Their faces remained stoic. One eased his pony forward. "The Kiowa come in friendship. No trouble. No guns."

Bill nodded. "No trouble. But yesterday, I say to the Kiowa that the woman was not for sale. She's my woman."

The Kiowa spokesman kept his eyes on Bill. "What does the woman say? She must decide."

"No. She has nothing to say. She—"

Millie's sharp voice cut him off. "I have every right to speak for myself."

Every eye in the camp snapped around, and every eye in camp bulged when they saw the diminutive woman standing in the rear of the Conestoga.

Her red hair was plastered to her head with the black grease from the tallow pot, and when she opened her mouth to speak, she appeared to be missing several teeth. Dark bags sagged under her cheeks, and deep lines wrinkled her forehead and cheeks. Her clothes were rags.

She had aged forty years in eight hours.

Slowly she climbed to the ground, and with the aid of a walking stick, hobbled to the fire.

The Kiowa braves looked at each other in shock.

Bill's jaw bounced off the ground.

Snag Podecker poured coffee in his lap.

Catman swallowed his tobacco.

And Pancake dumped sourdough in the coffeepot.

Millie staggered to a halt by the fire and squinted up at the Kiowa spokesman. "This the man who's lucky enough to get me for only twenty-four horses?'' she asked in a cracking, quavering voice.

The brave looked in horror at Bill, who simply shrugged. He didn't have the slightest idea what was going on. At a complete loss for words, he nodded and pointed to the Kiowa brave.

One Kiowa in the rear jabbered. The spokesman looked around and replied.

Another Kiowa shook his head and made a cutting motion with his hand. He wheeled his pony around and headed back to the remuda. The others followed.

Only the spokesman remained. He studied Millie for several moments, then looked at Bill sympathetically. ''You right. She your woman.'' And he hurried from the camp.

No one spoke for several seconds, then Snag Podecker drawled. ''Well, ma'am. It appears you ain't even worth a Winchester '76 anymore.''

A broad grin split her face, revealing black tar on her teeth. She wiped it away with a handkerchief. ''It does at that. Now, I need hot water for a hot bath.'' She held her hands out to her side. ''I'm not budging an inch until I'm clean.'' She fixed Bill Merritt with a withering look. ''I got us out of the mess you started. Now, you and this herd can wait until I've had my bath.''

Alwilda and Linitta watched from the Conestoga, their hands covering the smile on their lips.

Bill looked around, but his punchers were studying the sky or the ground, avoiding his eyes. This was a decision he was going to have to make on his own.

Pancake didn't give him the chance. ''Yes, ma'am. We'll boil water in the spiders and fix you up with a nice hot bath. Ain't that right, Mr. Merritt?''

"Huh? Oh, yeah. I . . . I reckon so. Besides, the stock can use some grazing time."

The Bar Slash continued its slow progress across Indian Territory, and in early October, the herd crossed the Canadian River and angled northwest toward Dodge. The nights had become somewhat cooler, although during the day the sun still scorched the prairie and blistered their necks.

The girls and Millie became accomplished riders, some days spending several hours in the saddle. On occasion, Alkali took Linitta and Alwilda under his wing and let them ride flank.

"You know, boss," Alkali drawled as they ambled across the prairie at point one afternoon, "the women sorta fit in now, don't they? Even the little half-pints. I mean, they learned what they needed to do, and they ain't been too much in the way."

"Reckon that's true. It's been a surprise to me, but I guess any jasper can learn." He nodded in their direction. "And you're right. They've picked up on things real fast."

That night around the fire, Linitta sat beside the rancher and balanced her plate of beef and beans in her lap. "How much longer before we reach Dodge City, Uncle Bill?"

He grinned. "Why? You gettin' tired of Pancake's grub?"

"Oh, no. I like Mr. Pancake's food . . . I mean, grub. I just wondered how much longer before it was over."

Bill sopped the last of his beans with a chunk of sourdough. "We're getting close. A couple weeks, I figure, give or take a few days."

"Oh." Linitta sighed. "That's not much time. I wish it was longer. If I was back home, I'd be in school now."

School? Bill paused, holding the dripping biscuit just beyond his lips. Blast if she wasn't right. It was time for the kids to be in school. That was another reason the girls needed to be back in Boston. They had to have an education.

"Well, it won't be too long before you're back in school. Your aunt's due back in Boston soon."

Linitta grew silent. Bill cleaned his plate with the last of his biscuit and sipped at his coffee.

"Uncle Bill?"

He looked down at the small girl. The sun had lightened her hair and tanned her face. Her blue eyes sparkled like fresh water. In her jeans and plaid shirt, she looked as if she'd been born a Texan. "Yeah?"

"Do we have to go back to Boston? I mean, couldn't we stay out here?"

Her questions caught the rawboned rancher off guard. He stammered. "I thought you wanted to go back. Alwilda does."

She ducked her head and picked at her food. "I know. But that was before I started helping Mr. Pancake and all. Alwilda can go back if she wants to."

Bill had not anticipated these feelings.

"But what about your aunt?"

Linitta shrugged. "Aunt Maude wouldn't care. She always liked Alwilda best anyway." She looked up at him hopefully.

"Well, I . . . I . . ." He squirmed uncomfortably. "I mean, something like that, we'd have to talk about. I just always figured you girls would hightail it to Boston when your Aunt Maude got back. I never thought about you staying here.''

Her bottom lip quivered. ''Oh,'' was all she said. She dropped her head and stared at the plate in her lap.

He looked down at her for several seconds, trying to find the right words to ease the hurt he had heaped on her. Finding none, he sighed, rose to his feet, and dropped his utensils in the washtub. He wished they would hit Dodge City tomorrow. He'd put Millie and the girls on the first train for Boston, and then he wouldn't have to worry about them any longer.

Usually a sound sleeper, Bill slept but little that night. To his surprise, he realized that he had grown fond of Millie and Linitta, and yes, even of the pain-in-the-neck Alwilda. He rose and picked his way through the slumbering cowpokes to the banked campfire, where he poured a cup of coffee. Pancake's coffee was always thick, but this had boiled down until it was like sorghum molasses, and with enough kick to wobble a jasper's eyeballs.

For the next hour, he squatted and stared at the darkened Conestoga. How simple his life had been before those three dainty little women came in. All he had to worry about then were Comanches, rustlers, hurricanes, and cottonmouths.

The herd continued across the rolling prairie, leaving Indian Territory and crossing into Kansas. One day, Bill was conspicious by his absence at the evening meal. ''I reckon he's scouting ahead,'' Snag said when Millie questioned the rancher's whereabouts. ''We been in Injun country, and now we're hittin' the Jayhawkers. Can't be none too careful around here. Especially since we're only a few days from Dodge.''

But Bill had been deliberately avoiding the women, trying to distance himself from them and not even understanding the reason for his behavior himself.

He kept telling himself that the West was no place for greenhorns, for children. Sure, he planned on marrying someday and raising a family, but such a drastic move was far down the road. Right now, life was too dangerous to even consider a family.

The sooner Millie and the girls got back to Boston, the better off they would be. And the sooner he sold his cattle, the sooner he could get back to Cibolo Springs.

The evening of their first day into Kansas, Bill sat in the saddle staring across the rolling prairie at the plodding herd. He patted Bumpo's neck. ''I made me a decision, Bumpo. Those girls are dandy little fillies. It don't seem right they go back to Boston with nothing, so I figured on turning down that lawyer Harper's offer on the ranch. I'll keep my half, and the girls can have Frank's.''

He hesitated and stared down at the back of Bumpo's head. He was proud of himself. He had spent days worrying over this quandary. Now, he had solved it. Now he could send the girls back to Boston without feeling guilty. Thanks to him, they'd be well taken care of.

And later, if they wanted to pay a visit, they could. Shoot, when they grew up, they could come back to Texas if they still wanted to. They could even live out here as far as he was concerned.

''Yeah,'' he muttered, giving Bumpo an extra sharp slap on the neck. ''I reckon that'll work out just fine. Don't you?''

Bumpo snorted and jerked at the reins. He twisted his head around and tried to bite Bill, who yanked the reins at the last second. "Hey! You blasted jughead. What the blazes is wrong with you?" He glared at the stallion, which was tossing his head. "Hardheaded, spavined gluepot."

On the way back to the herd, instead of his usual running walk, Bumpo dropped into a foxtrot, a broken, uncollected trot that jarred Bill from his toes to his teeth. Bill tried to increase the stallion's gait, but Bumpo stubbornly held his pace. When Bill tried to turn the roan to the right, Bumpo fought for the left. When he headed left, the stallion struggled to the right.

By the time they reached the remuda, Bill was ready to bust an ax handle over the animal's head. He dismounted and yanked the saddle from Bumpo, blistering the air with a tirade of brand-new invectives while Swede looked on in surprise.

As the rawboned rancher stomped away, Bumpo kicked at him.

Bill spun and pointed his finger at the belligerent horse. "You knock-kneed piece of crowbait! You'd better be mighty glad you didn't catch me with that foot or you'd be out there feeding the coyotes."

Bumpo stared at Bill.

Bill glared at Bumpo.

And Swede looked on in amazement.

Word spread through the camp, and next morning when Bill went out to the remuda, every eye in camp was skinned back, watching to see what would happen when the rancher tried to saddle Bumpo.

Bill shook out a loop and in a swift, clean toss caught

the black, disappointing everyone who had managed to hang around to watch the fun.

"Keep 'em moving, Alkali. I'm heading into Dodge to line up some buyers and set up pens. I'll meet you tonight in camp."

Alkali swung into his saddle and touched his fingers to the brim of his hat. "Get us a good price, boss."

"Do my best," Bill replied, swinging the black around and heading for Dodge. The first thing he planned to do when he hit town was line up train tickets for Millie and the girls and wire lawyer Harper about his change of mind. Then he would find a buyer for the beef.

At noon he rode into Dodge City, a wide-open cattle town catering to the wild and woolly cowpokes up from Texas. The streets bustled with activity, wagons and horses, women and children, drunken cowboys and stiff-necked businessmen.

Within an hour, he'd made all his arrangements and was headed back to the herd with half a dozen bottles of Old Crow in his saddlebags. Three tonight, and three tomorrow night, their last night on the trail.

As he rode out of town, three men stepped through the swinging doors of the Long Branch saloon and paused on the boardwalk, their eyes on the receding figure of Bill Merritt.

Chapter Eighteen

"Whhoooeee!" Alkali shouted when Bill revealed the terms of the sale. "Sixty thousand! I swear, I didn't know there was that much money in the world."

Bill glanced around the fire at the grinning faces of the punchers. "Yep. Feller from the Chicago Stockyards guaranteed it. We push the Bar Slashes into his pens and get to his office, and he'll count out the greenbacks right then and there. I reckon, that'll provide a nice little bonus for ever'one."

A chorus of laughter greeted his last remark.

Bill glanced at Millie, who was seated across the fire from him. She smiled, but there was a touch of sadness in it.

Later, Bill knocked on the side of the Conestoga.

Millie stuck her head out the pucker hole.

"Sorry to wake you."

She shook her head and climbed out of the wagon. "I wasn't sleeping. None of us were. We were just lying here talking about the next few days."

Bill nodded. "That's . . . that's what I wanted to talk about."

She forced a smile. "Well, you're just about finished with us. I suppose you're glad now that you won't have a bunch of women to worry about," she said brightly.

The lanky rancher shuffled his boots. "Well, not exactly. You all weren't a bunch of trouble. In fact, we enjoyed having you with us.''

Millie laughed. ''Now, Mr. Merritt. You don't really expect me to believe that, do you?''

His ears burned and he grinned sheepishly. Why did these women always make him feel uncomfortable? ''No, ma'am, I don't reckon I do, but I mean it when I say, you wasn't a whole bunch of trouble. A little maybe, but not a bunch.''

She laughed. ''Well, Mr. Merritt, at least, you're honest.''

''Yes, ma'am. I try to be.'' He cleared his throat. ''I made reservations at the Wright House in Dodge for you and the girls. And I got train tickets for you back to Boston.''

A frown knit her forehead. ''What about Harper? Aren't you going to wait for him and sign some papers about the ranch? After all, you lived up to your end of it.''

''I sent him a telegram. I changed my mind.'' He explained his decision about the ranch and the girls. ''I'm not the most honest hombre around. I been known to sneak a little here and there, but the girls are family. I won't take from them.''

She pushed her long red hair from her forehead. ''I don't understand. At first, you were all for it.''

Bill reached down and pulled up a stem of grama grass. He stuck it between his lips and chewed on it. ''Well, it's sorta like this. Frank and me never got along. We was brothers, but we didn't like each other especially. Him I could've taken the ranch from and never looked back. But the girls, they're kinda like snow, all nice and clean, never hurt nobody. They don't deserve a kick in the teeth. No, ma'am, it just isn't right to take what their pa left them.''

''But their Aunt Maude has money. They'll be well taken care of.''

Bill shrugged. ''Maybe so, but this way, the girls have something of their own.'' He hesitated, then added, his tone becoming reflective. ''It does something to a body if he has to depend on someone else. I don't want the girls to face that.''

A tear glistened in Millie's eye, and she laid her hand on his arm. ''You're a good man, Mr. Merritt.''

He chuckled. ''I reckon this cattle drive has kept you out in the sun too much, Miss Millie. You're kinda touched in the head.''

Two days later, the Bar Slashes crossed the Arkansas River and pushed into Dodge City, right down the middle of main street between the row of false-fronted buildings and the railroad tracks. Bill still rode the black, having completely ignored Bumpo the last couple days.

Ramón pulled up in front of the Wright House and helped the women inside, where the first luxury they called for was a hot bath.

Ten minutes after the punchers had closed the gate on the last beef, Bill and Alkali walked out of the Cattleman's Association Building with sixty thousand dollars tucked in a belt around Bill's waist. Shorty, Snag, and the other hands were waiting on the boardwalk.

Alkali rubbed his hands together. ''I can sure use a drink, boss. Can't you, fellers?''

They shouted their agreement.

Bill nodded to the Long Branch Saloon. ''I reckon over yonder is as good a place to settle up as anywhere.''

He paused on the steps in front of the saloon and addressed his men. "Each of you got your pay and a pony coming. I'm selling everything else and heading back to Cibolo Springs tomorrow. Without wagons, I figure to make it in a couple weeks. Any jasper who wants to ride along is welcome. Be sure to stock up on grub. Now, come on inside and get your pay. The first round's on me."

After receiving their pay, some of the drovers bellied up to the bar. Two or three headed for the local tonsorial parlor for a haircut, shave, and bath. Still others roamed the street, taking in the sights.

Bill sat at a rear table in the saloon, nursing his first drink, his mind on Millie and the girls. They had everything they needed. He'd made all of the arrangements, room, tickets, funds. There was no practical reason for him to see them, but he couldn't leave without saying good-bye. After all, he reminded himself, the same blood in his veins was in theirs.

A guttural voice interrupted his thoughts. "Howdy, Mr. Merritt."

He looked up into the bearded face of a man who looked strangely familiar. "Do I know you?"

The man's eyes were cold and lifeless. A sneer curled his lips and his breath reeked of stale cigars and cheap whiskey. "No reason you should remember. I brought word from an old friend of yours."

An uncomfortable itch began nagging at the base of Bill's skull. "Yeah? And who might that be?"

"Waco Brown."

Bill stiffened.

Before he could reply, the hardcase handed him a note. "Do what it says, or you'll be sorry."

The rawboned rancher opened the note and quickly read it.

You ever want to see that woman and them girls again, bring me sixty thousand dollars tonight at midnight at the big bend of the Arkansas north of town. Come alone and don't tell nobody.

Bill looked up, but the hardcase had disappeared.

"What are you goin' to do, boss?" Alkali asked.

He stood on the steps of the Wright House after searching Millie and the girls' rooms. "Not much choice." He studied the faces looking up at him, dark, angry faces ready to slap leather and put someone in Boot Hill. "Do what they say."

Catman tore off a chunk of tobacco and deposited it in his cheek. "Can't trust skunks like that, Bill. Maybe we need to put us some scouts out and follow them once they git the money."

"I studied on that." He hooked his thumb over his shoulder. "Nobody in there knows a thing. Those hombres sneaked the women out of the hotel right under everyone's nose, slicker'n bear grease. You're right. We can't trust them."

Snag spoke up. "Catman's right, boss. You got to go in alone, but after dark, the rest of us need to spread ourselves around so we can tag along after those galoots and get your money back."

"Sounds good to me," Shorty and Pump chimed in.

Bill studied his men. "I can't figure any other way myself. So let's do it like you say." He scanned the busy street. "They're probably out there watching now. So let's break up. They know you been paid off. Some might head south out of town. Cross the river and strike out for Texas. The rest of you drift around town, try to lose yourself in the crowd, but be in place by ten o'clock tonight.''

After the men had spread, Alkali shucked his six-gun and inspected the cylinder. ''You ain't got sixty thousand, boss. Not after ever'one was paid.''

''I got enough. Besides, we don't plan on letting them keep it, do we?''

Alkali chuckled. ''Reckon not.'' He looked at Bill. ''Something else on your mind, boss?''

''I'm not sure. But I got the feeling we're forgetting something.''

Clouds rolled in, smothering the light from the crescent moon. Occasionally, the clouds parted and a shaft of moonlight jabbed at the ground. Objects along the road appeared as darker shadows, black on black.

On the outskirts of Dodge, Bill paused and laid his hand on the money belt around his waist. He looked down at Bumpo. The stallion had not moved a muscle when the rancher saddled him. It was as if he knew their contest of wills had to be pushed aside for the time being, that there was serious work to be done. ''Okay, boy. We can't see them, but we got friends out there.'' He clicked his tongue. ''Now, let's you and me do our part.''

Earlier in the day, he had ridden the black out to the bend to familiarize himself with the lay of the land. He had to be prepared for anything. So now he headed out the north road. At the first bend, he cut directly toward the river.

The clouds had thickened. Bill could barely see the

ground at his feet. He had to trust Bumpo's instincts. Then he smelled the river.

A light flashed ahead of him. It flashed again. Without being told, Bumpo headed for the light. The ground began dropping away to the shore, and now Bill could hear the swishing and gurgling of the rolling river.

A disembodied voice came from the darkness. "That's far enough."

"Whoa, boy." Bill strained his eyes to penetrate the darkness. At that moment, the clouds broke, revealing a ferry tied to the shore. At first, he didn't understand the significance of the raftlike vessel, and then his blood ran cold. The one thing he hadn't planned on. The one thing he had forgotten.

The lantern came toward him. A hand took Bumpo's reins, and the lantern went out. "Just sit still, mister. No one will get hurt. Drop your gun."

Bill did as he was told.

Bumpo was led onto the ferry. "Get down."

The rancher climbed down. The vessel lurched under his feet, and he felt it begin to move. He glanced over his shoulder. A guttural voice laughed. "Them cowpokes of yours ain't gonna be no help."

A shadow came toward him. "We're taking you for a little ride. You got the money?"

Bill recognized the voice. Waco Brown. "Where are the women?"

"We got 'em. Let's see the money first."

"I got the money. You'll get it when I see them."

A voice in the darkness beside him growled. "Let's take it, Waco."

"Naw. He ain't going nowhere. They're over there, at the end of the raft."

Bill's eyes had grown accustomed to the dark, and he spotted a bulky object several feet away. When he reached it, he discovered it was a tarp. He pulled it away. Millie and the girls were bound and gagged.

The clouds broke, and Bill could see the fear in the girls' eyes. A surge of anger coursed through his veins. He fought to control his voice. "Take it easy, girls. Everything's okay."

"That's enough palavering. Where's the money?"

Rising quickly, Bill removed the moneybelt and tossed it to Waco Brown, "Here." He knelt and quickly freed the women. Alwilda threw her arms around his neck and sobbed. The rawboned rancher grabbed her shoulders and held her at arm's length. He spoke gently, but his meaning was clear. "Don't cry. This is not the time. You understand?"

Alwilda sniffled and shook her head.

"Good." Bill stood and faced the kidnappers. There were four. "You got the money. Now, put us ashore."

With the moneybelt in his hand, Brown stepped forward and snarled. "I told you I'd get you. There ain't no jail that can keep Waco Brown, and there ain't no man alive who can brag he got the best of me."

Bill remained silent. A cold resolve settled over him. He glanced at Millie and the girls, for just as he knew what the outlaw had in mind for him, he also knew what Waco Brown had planned for the women.

There was a sudden movement at his side. Bill jerked away, but his head exploded with brilliant lights as a gun muzzle clipped him on the side of the head, knocking him to the deck. He tried to move, but his muscles refused to listen. His hand hung limply in the water.

The hardcase that had poleaxed him laughed and bent

over. "Get up, cowboy. I want you to bleed real good before I croak you."

A child's voice cut through the darkness. "You stop hurting my uncle," Linitta shouted.

Before the owlhoot could move, she ran up and gave him a hard shove in the rear. Bent over, he lost his balance and lunged forward, headfirst, into the swirling waters.

"What the . . ." Waco Brown spun and aimed a kick at the girl, but Bill rolled over and slammed the heel of his boots into Brown's knee.

Millie and Alwilda jumped into the fray.

Alwilda grabbed one outlaw by the leg and promptly started gnawing on his calf. He jumped around on one foot, trying to shake her off the other. "You blasted kid. I'm gonna whop you good as soon . . ."

Bill popped him in the temple with a bony fist, and the man dropped like a dead steer.

Linitta and Millie were clawing and scratching Waco Brown, who was rolling across the decking cursing and shouting.

The fourth owlhoot grabbed Bill and jammed a gun in his belly. "Call 'em off. Call 'em off, or you're dead."

For a fleeting moment, Bill started to refuse, but just as quickly, he agreed. The outlaw jerked him to his feet. "Now, do it. Call 'em off."

But before Bill could say a word, Bumpo bared his teeth and clamped his incisors into the owlhoot's shoulder and yanked back. With a scream of agony, the outlaw dropped his six-gun and grabbed his shoulder. Bill stepped forward and slammed a knotted fist into the outlaw's jaw, knocking him into the river.

On the far side of the vessel, Waco Brown climbed to

his feet. Linitta clung to one leg while Millie tried to yank the moneybelt from Brown's grasp. With his free hand, he shucked his six-gun and struck Linitta on the head with a glancing blow. Then he swung the muzzle toward Millie.

Bill lunged and hit Brown in the middle of the chest with his shoulder, spilling both men into the swirling river. He grabbed for the six-gun with both hands as they rolled over and over underwater.

Brown's fingers dug into his eyes, but Bill shook his head and tried to rip the six-gun from the outlaw's grasp. Water poured down his throat. He coughed and sputtered, but maintained his grip on Brown's wrist.

They burst to the surface. Bill sucked in a lungful of fresh air and threw a straight right at the outlaw's face. His fist bounced off Brown's forehead, stunning the man long enough for Bill to knock the revolver from the outlaw's hand. The river forced them toward the shore.

With a shout of anger, Waco Brown grabbed Bill's throat, but Bill knocked his hands aside and slammed another fist into the man's forehead. His feet touched bottom, and before the outlaw Brown could attack, the rawboned rancher planted his feet and threw a left cross that whistled through the air.

Brown dipped his head, and the punch flew harmlessly past. He leaped at Bill and dug his clawlike fingers into the rancher's neck, knocking him back into the water. The current pulled them under, bouncing them along the muddy bottom.

Flashing lights exploded in Bill's head, and a great roaring filled his ears. He clawed at the outlaw's face, jabbing his finger's into Brown's eyes, at the same time scrabbling around in an effort to get his feet under him.

His heels caught in the mud, and he pushed himself erect, yanking both himself and Brown from the water. Sweeping his arms upward, he tore the outlaw's hands from about his throat. Gasping for breath, Bill threw his shoulders into a left hook, catching the outlaw on the jaw, snapping his head around.

Brown spun and fell forward in the water.

Bill stumbled after him, but the current sucked the rustler and kidnapper under, out of reach.

He heard his name. A dark object loomed in the river behind him. "Bill! Where are you?"

"Here," he managed to shout. "Over here."

A rope whistled out of the darkness and struck him across the face. He winced and muttered a curse.

Alwilda called out. "Did you get the rope, Uncle Bill? I threw it to you."

Bill pulled himself to the raft. "I could have guessed that," he muttered, his face stinging.

Moments later, he climbed aboard the raft.

The clouds broke, lighting the raft like a halo. The girls hugged Bill, and he hugged them. Millie stood apart. Bill grinned. "You might as well come here. You're part of this family whether you like it or not."

With a squeal of delight, Millie joined the family.

"The only problem is, we're broke. All our money is at the bottom of the river."

"Oh, you mean this," Millie said innocently, holding up the moneybelt.

Bill shook his head and hugged the girls to him. "Well, girls, it looks like we got us quite a woman here.

The only question is, do you think I can talk her into marrying me, and being a mother to you girls back in Texas?''

Millie and the girls stared at him in surprise. Bill grinned. Finally, he had found a way to keep them quiet, for a few minutes at least.